The Remarkable & Very True Story of Lucy & Snowcap

The Remarkable
& Very True
Story
of
Lucy
& Snowcap

H.M. Bouwman

MARSHALL CAVENDISH CHILDREN

Marshall Cavendish Corporation

99 White Plains Road

Tarrytown, NY 10591

www.marshallcavendish.us/kids

This book is a work of fiction. Names, characters, places, and incidents are products of the author's
imagination and are used fictitiously. Any resemblance to actual events or locales or persons,
living or dead, is entirely coincidental.

Library of Congress Cataloging-in-Publication Data

Bouwman, H. M.

The remarkable and very true story of Lucy and Snowcap / by H.M. Bouwman.

– 1st ed.

p. cm.

Summary: In 1787, twelve years after English convicts are shipwrecked on
the magical islands of Tathenland, two twelve-year-old girls, one a native
Colay, the other the child-governor of the English, set out on a journey to
stop the treachery from which both peoples are suffering.

ISBN 978-0-7614-5441-0

[1. Adventure and adventurers–Fiction. 2. Colonists–Fiction. 3.
Magic–Fiction. 4. Babies–Fiction. 5. Islands–Fiction.] I. Title.

PZ7.B6713Rem 2008

[Fic]–dc22

20080031

Interior artwork on pages 41, 47, 77, 118, and 130 by Megan McNinch

Editor: Robin Benjamin

Printed in China

First edition

10 9 8 7 6 5 4 3 2 1

mc Marshall Cavendish
Children

For

Rob, Adam, Jesse, Emily, Henry, Josiah, Gabriel,
Elijah, Wyatt, Edison, Katie, Klara, Rafael,
Quentin, Mitchell, Norah, and Corinne.

With deep thanks to:

Swati Avasthi, Lisa Bullard, Heather Goodman,
Pete Hautman, Marilyn Mark, Bob Parker,
Rick Powers, Scott Wrobel, and the remarkable
Robin Benjamin.

*I have forgotten more
than mere continents.
The places I remember
are lost from the map.
I will tell you a story
of one of these places.*

—FROM THE JOURNAL OF PHILIP TUTOR, 1790

TABLE OF CONTENTS

A Timeline of the English in Tathenland
by Philip the Tutor
Spring 1788

1774-75:
255 prisoners in England are convicted of crimes and sentenced to transportation.

1775, early spring:
The 255 prisoners are incarcerated on three ships bound for America, where they will be sold as indentured servants.

1775, late spring:
The three ships, after a long storm, are shipwrecked on a group of islands somewhere north and east (we think) of the American colonies. 236 of the prisoners survive and come ashore. Robert O'Kelly is elected Governor of the islands, which are declared a new colony of Britain and named Tathenland (its largest island is Tathenn). The natives (the Colay) are informed that they are now subjects of the King.

1775, early summer:
The first English baby is born—the Governor's golden daughter, Snowcap O'Kelly—in Baytown (formerly called Picle), on the main island (now called the mainland) of Tathenn. The same month, a mostly unremarkable Colay child is born on the island of Sunset: Lucy, daughter of Del and Dara.

1786, early summer:
Governor and Mrs. O'Kelly die. A few months later, Sir
Markham (the Protector—the acting Governor) and
Renard (the steward) investigate and conclude that
the Colay are to blame and are fomenting a rebellion. The
Colay are banned from Tathenn. (The desert Colay are left
alone as they seem to be unconnected to the Rebellion and,
in addition, are hard to reach.) In fact, the Colay are not
merely confined to their islands, but are turned to stone.
To stone!

Oh, dear. The story needs far more detail than an outline
can lend. It is a _story_, after all, and it should be told
like one.

The Remarkable &
Very True Story
of Lucy & Snowcap

1

TO THE LIFESTONE GARDEN

(EARLY SUMMER, 1787)

The midwife told Lucy to take her newborn brother to the Lifestone Garden and leave him there to die.

Lucy had known this might happen, but still she hadn't really expected it, had even wished against it, though she never would have admitted that kind of weakness to anyone. As if wishing could change anything. Climbing the mountain to the garden, she thought back on the long events of this long day—how it all might have gone differently, if only the baby had been a girl or if the Colay didn't live on cursed islands or if they *weren't* Colay or if the Anglish had never come to their land. Then this might have been a good day, and she wouldn't be walking up the mountain now, carrying her new brother to the garden to die.

Early that morning, Lucy's mother had sent her to fetch the midwife. Bastia came—old, wide, and humped, slow moving and slow talking—carrying her basket of medicines and shooing Lucy away from the hut when the two of them arrived. "Go on, now, girl! I'll call you when I need you." Bastia thumped inside the hut. "Dara, it's time today, is it? How do you feel?"

Lucy sat down outside, leaning her back against the hut and scowling into the sun. *Sent away like a child—like I don't matter*, she thought. To make everything worse, a moment later she overheard two girls her age walking past. One said nervously, "Oh, I hope it lives! I hope it's a girl!" and the other elbowed her friend and said, "I hope the poor thing doesn't look like Lucy! Only imagine!" They both dissolved in giggles. When they saw Lucy sitting motionless and staring, they stopped short, bowed their heads, and scurried away. She glared after them. Although in many ways she resembled the other Colay children, with thick black hair and brown skin and a strong, stocky body, Lucy knew nonetheless that she wasn't pretty—she was ungraceful and clunky, with her hair always sticking up. *Even without the mark on my face I'd be plain*, she thought. But with the mark, she was just plain ugly.

Shortly after Bastia went into the hut, the neighbors began to gather nearby. The first woman to reach the hut asked Lucy, "Is it her time?"

Another woman ran up. "Oh, will it be today?" She twisted her fingers in her tunic. "Do you think—

do you think—a boy or a girl?"

"One or the other," snapped Lucy, and the first woman muttered, "Rude."

Before Lucy could respond, Bastia poked her head out of the hut and asked for water. "Quickly, child," she said brusquely and pulled her head back in. Lucy stood up.

More women had walked up to the hut, and several girls, little and big. "What's this?" said one of the women. "The girl hasn't fetched the water yet?" She turned to the woman next to her. "When my Salter was born, my eldest fetched water every morning, just in case I was having the baby that day. When I finally did give birth, water filled every pot in the yard!"

"Yes, and where's Salter now?" said Lucy, only half under her breath.

"What was that?" The woman whipped her head toward Lucy.

A little girl piped up. "She said where's Salt—"

Lucy elbowed the little girl, who tripped forward, gasping. Lucy swung her buckets vigorously, and the girls closest to her stepped out of range. "I said, I'll go get the water now." She headed for the spring.

When she returned with full buckets, she found all the women, even Bastia, talking about her, their backs turned as she walked into the clearing. Salter's mother was crying so that her voice creaked. "How dare she?"

Aunt Fern, who had no children anymore, was protective of her niece. "Don't mind Lucy. She's only a child. And this is a hard time for her."

Bastia snorted. "Her? She's never been a child."

"And it's a hard time for us all!" said a young woman carrying a small girl on her hip. "That girl's just a world of trouble. And no feelings at all. There's something wrong with her. It's not just her face."

"I'm back," said Lucy, and they all stopped talking and looked at her.

"Lucy?" Aunt Fern said gently. "Come here, child—"

"It doesn't matter," said Lucy. "I don't care what people say."

Aunt Fern frowned, and Lucy heard a woman murmur, "She doesn't care about anything," and another replied, "Stone heart."

"I don't care," Lucy said again, louder. "And stone hearts don't get hurt." She glared around her, and one of the women ducked her head, embarrassed.

Good! They should know better than to gossip about me.

Lucy's mother called gently from the hut, breathing hard through her words, "Let—Lucy—be. She's a plain talker. That's—her person."

"There's plain talk, and there's outright rudeness," Bastia said. She was answering Dara but looking at Lucy. "Don't be surly, miss. Just give me the water. And don't glare."

"If people call me names, I'll glare." Lucy put the buckets down and strode off.

At the beach she put her hand up to her throat, as she often did these days, and felt the empty pouch that hung on a string around her neck. Every Colay had a luck pouch. Babies were given a pouch with one special item in it, secret and invested with meaning, and they added to it as they grew up. Everyone treasured their pouch; a luck pouch keeps you safe, the elders said. Its power comes from your island, tethers you always to the land.

But eight months ago, when everything went so

horribly wrong and Lucy feared she was to blame, she had emptied out her pouch into the sea. It had been filled with solid, hopeful things: her birth present, a tiny feather her mother had found the day Lucy was born; a red, almost-glowing stone Lucy had stumbled on at the beach one day; a walnut her father had carved into a little, perfect face; a small bundle of pungent herbs that grew only on her island; and a string from her first fish-net. These things were all important to her and her alone. And now they were gone—as she remembered every time she felt the flat pouch.

Lucy stayed at the beach and threw stones until the sun was high in the sky, and then threw more stones until the sun was low again and her shoulders ached. No one came and found her, though she half hoped they might. She told herself that it didn't matter and that she didn't want to know about the baby until it was all over, anyway. But in the end, she had to trudge back to the hut. She couldn't stay away any longer, and she was tired of trying not to cry.

Better just to go and find out the truth.

By the time Lucy arrived, everyone in the village was waiting outside to learn the news—for they knew that this would be the last baby born on Sunset. Lucy sat down and joined the waiting, and several girls moved over to give her space.

Because they were all so quiet, when the baby was born they heard its first gasp of air, its first cry. There was a short silence, and then Lucy's mother said "no" rather loudly and started crying, very softly. It sounded odd to Lucy, not only because her mother never, ever cried—not even when all the men and boys had disappeared—but also because the "no" was so loud next to her mother's soft crying, almost as if the sounds were from two different people. But there was no more time to think about it, for Bastia came out of the hut, and everyone wanted to know what she would say.

Bastia stood in the doorway and folded her arms over her large chest.

"A boy."

Then she turned and went back into the hut.

Everyone was silent, even the littlest girls. Everyone was scared.

A few minutes later, Bastia brought the baby outside. He was wrapped in a blanket, tiny and pale in her wide brown arms. Bastia held him up without expression and said, "His name is Robert, after the dead Anglish Governor, who was a good man. Take a look now at the last baby of Sunset."

Lucy squinted at the squirmy bundle. Not impressive, really. What the others thought about her brother she couldn't tell, for no one spoke, not even her mother, still crying softly and invisibly inside the hut. Then Aunt Fern asked slowly, "Bastia, will he fulfill the promise? Will he fulfill the prophecy and save us? Or will he . . . ?"

Bastia looked at the anxious faces. "I don't know," she said. Then her shoulders sagged, and she looked tired. "I'm just an old woman who doesn't know anything. But take a close look. No more pregnant women here. This is the last baby."

Most of the women were crying as they gathered around Bastia to see the red and wrinkled baby boy, his eyes pressed shut and fists curled as if protesting being born. Bastia sat on the ground and laid the baby on her lap. She unwrapped his blankets.

Everyone pressed closer, but no one touched him.

Lucy, who had been sitting in the back with the other girls, now pushed and poked and wriggled her way to the front. She wanted to see the baby—he was her brother, after all. Aunt Fern, eyeing the women being poked and the girls having their toes stepped on, said, "Let Lucy in." The women rustled and parted like waves to let Lucy slip through. As she neared Bastia, Lucy heard the midwife murmur, "A beautiful baby."

"So perfect," added another woman.

"Doesn't look at all like—"

"Yes," agreed Bastia. "Special."

Circled by the sea of women, Lucy reached Bastia and hovered at her shoulder. She watched as Bastia bent over the baby and took off all his swaddling. "Now we will see," said Bastia. Tentatively she touched the baby's face, his hands, his arms. She touched his chest, his stomach as it rippled quickly up and down.

"What are you doing?" Lucy asked, even though she knew. No one answered.

"Does he breathe?" one of the women asked.

"He breathes," Bastia replied.

"He seems healthy," said another, but there was doubt in her voice.

"What are you doing?" Lucy asked, louder.

Bastia touched his legs. She touched his right foot. Then his left. Gasped. The women pressed closer, still without touching the baby themselves. "What is it? What's wrong?" Their quiet voices were edged with panic.

"What? What?" asked Lucy, pulling on Bastia's arm.

She knew her mother would have scolded her for talking to an elder in such a rude tone, but Lucy needed to know what was happening. She needed to know the truth.

Bastia didn't answer. She touched the baby's left foot again. And again. *And again.* Bastia shook her head, and Lucy could see now that she was crying, too.

"Is it . . . ?" one woman began.

Bastia nodded. "It's cold. His foot is cold."

The women were all crying openly now, and some of the little girls were joining in. Bastia bundled the baby again in his blanket. Then she turned to Lucy. "We can't keep him. Take him to the garden and leave him. There will be no baby." Her tone was almost brisk, and her eyes did not meet Lucy's. She held out the baby.

Aunt Fern reached as if to push the baby back into Bastia's arms. "No. Lucy's too young to go there by herself."

But Lucy said, "I'll go." Her throat felt dry and tight, and her voice sounded funny.

"This child's not afraid to walk among statues," said Bastia. "She'll come out fine. Tough as goats' teeth, she is."

And, though she knew Bastia hadn't meant to give a compliment, Lucy felt as if she had received one. She was tough. Bastia said so. Her eyes burned with unshed tears, but she squinted so that no one would notice. She peeked into the hut to say good-bye to her mother, but Dara was quiet now, staring up at the ceiling, and did not acknowledge her daughter's presence. Lucy blinked her eyes hard and left, carrying the baby.

After a few minutes of walking, Lucy's eyes felt cooler and her throat less gritty. She paused on the path a short way up the Gray Mountain. Dusk had not quite fallen, the day still paling to a close as the sun slid down toward the faint line where the sky met the sea. Lucy held the swaddled baby in her arms and looked northeast, her back to the sun. Out of habit she named and counted the islands clustered near her own Sunset Island, even the ones she couldn't see, swallowed up by the horizon or blocked by nearer islands. There were thirteen Colay Islands. To the south, almost invisible in the late-afternoon haze, was the mainland of Tathenn, where many Colay used to live and raise crops before the Anglish arrived. Picle, the only town of any size on Tathenn, was still the center of trade, where Lucy's father used to sell fish and seaweed, first to Colay and later to Anglish merchants; it was where he planned to begin his new trading business—and where he had promised to take her on his next trip, his biggest trip ever. But the next trip never happened.

Lucy glowered and looked northeast again, at the Colay Islands. The lush, gentle mountains jutted out of the sea: songs were sung about them and stories told about how they rose at the dawn of time. But ever since the creation of the statue gardens, Lucy could no longer see the beauty in the islands. *No, the problems started before the gardens,* she reminded herself. *It was them.* Twelve years ago, just a month before her own birth, the Anglish had arrived from the east. *Everything is their doing,* she thought for the hundredth time; *all the emptiness on the islands is their doing. And this baby, too. Not my fault. Theirs.*

The baby made a muffled noise, and Lucy lifted the blanket and looked into his tearless baby eyes, his red, angry face. No doubt he was hungry. Bastia owned a small bladder shaped especially for a baby's mouth, but in everyone's hurry, no one had thought to give it to Lucy. Anyway, what was the point of feeding a baby that was not destined to live?

The baby kept fussing, so Lucy put her littlest finger in his mouth for him to suck. He didn't suck, but he did close his eyes and doze. His face relaxed—*such smooth skin!*—and Lucy lightly touched his warm forehead. When she pulled the blanket further back, she could see the dark curls on his head. Beautiful. Even Bastia had said so, and Bastia was not one to lie. She had never, for example, said that Lucy was beautiful.

Lucy frowned; the baby slept, but she could still hear weeping. She looked down at her village: small huts draped around a thin crescent-moon bay. Even from this distance, Lucy could hear the women and girls, and she could see their shapes clustered around her mother's hut. When Lucy left the village, all twenty-one of them had already begun the ritual wailing that marked funerals; this time, tinged with something more desperate. Everyone wailing, that is, except Lucy. Crying was a waste of time; what was going to happen was going to happen, and crying wouldn't take it away. *Stupid, really, to cry like that.* No one would catch her being so snivelly.

The wailing was getting louder. The noise might wake the baby, and if he woke up, *he'd* start crying again, too. Just what she needed. Better keep moving. She had to get to the garden before nightfall. Not that Lucy was afraid of the dark—*I'm not*, she told herself firmly—but she didn't want to go groping and crashing among the statues at night. She began climbing again, moving a little faster than before.

Lucy knew that the Lifestone Garden was the key to

understanding the unhappiness of all thirteen Colay Islands. Each island had its own Lifestone Garden, and each island was miserably sad. No one ever went to the gardens except to mourn. Lucy had been there only when the island women held memorial services and draped flowers on the statues. The services were dull affairs, full of pageantry and singing and pretty girls performing slow dances. All the women and girls of Sunset attended these services, which were invariably held on bright and sunny days and after which everyone ate soup and flatbread.

Under normal circumstances, Lucy would have wanted to play in such a garden, nestled as it was on a hillside full of flowers. She would have climbed the low-branched apple trees drooping with tart fruit; and perched on the life-sized statues; or played catch-the-goat among them with her cousins, Branch and Brady, the only village children whom she ever played with. The others were too dumb and childish for her (and it didn't help that they seemed to not want to play with her, either). Branch and Brady didn't usually mind her company, though they did have an infuriating habit of talking to each other with secret signs that she couldn't understand—sometimes even in Anglish.

But, anyway, these were not normal circumstances. The Lifestone Garden was a cursed garden. Frozen in the stones were people Lucy had known: the men and boys of Sunset. Two were her cousins Branch and Brady. Another was her father.

Everyone said *statues*. It was the only word they could think of, but it was inaccurate, for statues were chiseled and carved. Sculpted from stone. These were more like rocks that just happened to be in the shapes of people—perfectly formed, without any signs of carving. Statues only if statues could grow themselves, like flowers.

How had this happened? No one was certain. Lucy had an idea that if people learned about the Anglish trader, they might blame her father. And *her*. She couldn't tell anyone. Her father was the only one who would have understood, and he was gone.

People had different theories about what had happened, but all the theories boiled down to magic: the magic in the land had gotten into the men—in a bad way, like a luck pouch gone dreadfully wrong, its land-loving powers out of control and turned against the wearer.

Everyone knew there were certain places where strange things happened—where boats went awry, where lost objects turned up, where animals talked in almost-human ways—and everyone likewise knew that such magic should not be toyed with. You left it alone, and it (for the most part) left you alone. And unless you were destined to be a shaman—which had not happened in anyone's living memory—you did not converse with the magic. Aunt Fern's theory was that someone had tried not only to converse with it but to control it, and the stones had gotten angry. That it was a man who did this was beyond question, since the men had all been punished. No one even suspected that Lucy might be partly to blame.

Lucy didn't believe in magic. She did *not*. But she could not deny the evidence of the statues: the men and boys had been turned into stone somehow, into lifestone—the very stone that the Colay used for so many purposes—the very stone that Lucy's father had been planning to dig out and trade with the Anglish. And now the statues dotted the garden, immobile and eloquent.

Trudging along the path, Lucy shifted the sleeping baby in her arms. He was small and she was strong, but it was tiring to carry him all that way uphill. In fact, he seemed to grow heavier with each step. Suddenly a terrible thought struck her: *Maybe he is changing, right now, in my arms?* Impossible, but still . . . it had happened to the others. She had to see for herself. Sitting on a big rock that was hunched along the path, she laid the baby down and undid his blanket. He was dressed only in a little cloth folded around his bottom; his fists were tightly curled and his head tipped to one side in sleep. Lucy looked him over as carefully as Bastia had done earlier. His skin had the healthy glow of any normal Colay new-born. *Good.* Somewhat relieved, she picked up his hands. They were warm, and his arms moved easily. His stomach moved up and down with each breath. He looked so healthy and alive that Lucy had to touch his feet—just to make sure Bastia hadn't imagined it back in the village. No, it was true: his left foot was cool to the touch, and the sole of the foot was tinged white. But it didn't look any worse than it had back in the village. He was not growing heavier. *He isn't going to . . . Not yet,* she promised herself.

She wrapped him up and sat for a moment, the baby sleeping peacefully next to her. Stretching out her tired arms, Lucy looked back toward home. The path began at the west edge of the village and headed west, but it soon doubled back and headed east, and then doubled back again, and again, wriggling its way up the hill like a snake. Lucy and the baby were now high above the village, and she could see it spread out far below, small and grubby and insignificant in the fading light, the boats pulled in and the narrow fields deserted. One hut—her own—was lit, and dim figures remained gathered around it in the dusk.

Dusk. Lucy shook herself. She had to hurry to make it to the garden before night. It wasn't far now. She nestled the baby in her arms and set off once again, climbing uphill, followed by the windy, distant keening of twenty-one women and girls.

2

THE ANGLISH

On the day that the last baby of Sunset was born, the twelve-year-old Child Governor of Tathenn was having a difficult time. To begin with, she was hungry. She had refused her breakfast because Renard, the steward (who had been, among other things, a magician in London), had poisoned it while Sir Markham, the Protector, stood by the door and kept watch for him. She had witnessed the poisoning herself. In the wee hours of the morning, unable to sleep and prowling the house, she had seen them tiptoeing into the kitchen, followed them, and (hidden in the shadow of the pantry door) watched Renard powder her oatmeal with rat poison while Sir Markham hissed nervously for him to hurry. So she decided to forgo her breakfast that day, much to Renard's and Sir Markham's fury. She was glad to have outsmarted the vile duo, but the incident was still rather distressing. *Something must be done about those two*, she thought. *I can't always follow them.* She had to eat and sleep sometime.

At school she had, as was often the case, little opportunity to think. This morning the pupils were told to write a historical essay about a subject of their choosing. Thus it happened that on the morning that the women of Sunset were waiting for a baby, this English girl in Baytown (formerly Picle), on the mainland of Tathenn, sat at her desk; pulled back her long white-blonde hair so it wouldn't drag in the ink; and composed the following manuscript:

The Inhabitents of Tathenland
By Snowcap Margaret O'Kelly, Child Governor
June 1787

Before the English discovered it in 1775, Tathenland was compozed of two grupes of peeple: the Desert Colay and the Colay Islanders. The desert people live on the mane land of Tathenn, in the desert. Peple call them Filosofers I mean Philosofers because they are hermits who live together. They have herds of goats but no horses. The only horses here are the offsprings of the ones that the English brout over. These horses are beyoutiful, but the best one is my horse Peat. Peat is black and fast and very smart. He likes tart apples. Adam the groom takes care of him wile I am stuck in school. When I come to the stables Adam tells me stories about Lundon and teaches me how to take care of Peat.

The Remarkable & Very True Story of Lucy & Snowcap

The Colay Ilanders live on the little islands north
of Tathenn, and they are fishers and seaweed farmers.
They have some very small goats but no horses either.
The Colay Islands look very small and dreary from here
in Baytown—it used to be Picle, but the English named it
Baytown, wich is a better name.

The Desert Colay and the Colay Islanders are all
one peaple, not realy two grupes like I said. They just
live in two diffrent places. They like each other. But the
Colay islanders were horrible and killed lots of people
including my mother and my father the Governor but then
they didn't manage to get Sir Markham or Renard. This
is called the Rebellion. So they are not allowed to come
to Tathenn anymor. Soon only the desert peaple will be
left. And the English. And the horses.

This is who the residents of Tathenland were. Then
we English landed. That was one month before I was
born. And everything in Tathenland is diffrent now.

The end. By Snowcap Margaret O'Kelly, Child
Governer. I will reelly be Governor when I turn fifteen.

The head tutor at Baytown's school was Philip Parsons, a
gangly middle-aged man with lank brown hair that
wisped into nothing at his shoulders and a timid way of
walking with his elbows pulled in tight. Philip was one
of the few convicts (along with Sir Markham) who
had an education, so when the English organized on
Tathenn, he was offered the head tutor position. (And
Sir Markham became Secretary to Governor O'Kelly.)
Since Baytown was the capital of Tathenn, Philip really
did have quite an important job. He taught the Most-
Important Children in the colony. He happened to be
foppish, self-centered, and awkward with children (who

didn't like him much), but that was beside the point. The point was that he took his job seriously: he was careful to mark papers very strictly and not play favorites, not even with a Child Governor who was destined to become the true Governor of Tathenland one day.

It wasn't that Philip disliked Snowcap; in fact, he felt rather sorry for her because she, too, had no friends. And he admired her spirit, though he would never have told *her* that. But—he had high standards, and in this essay, Snowcap hadn't met them. So after he read her paper, Philip dipped his quill in a jar of red ink and wrote with large flourishes:

Rewrite. Your spelling is atrocious.

Philip's criticism was a bit unfair. Snowcap's spelling was certainly atrocious; she had no idea what a dictionary was, whereas Philip (who had been four years old when Samuel Johnson's esteemed dictionary was first published) believed in Spelling. But many people, Snowcap included, were perfectly comfortable with alternate spellings for words (one for every mood) and resented correction. Besides, none of the convicts had thought to bring Dr. Johnson's dictionary with them when they sailed from England on that fateful journey that left them shipwrecked on Tathenn. So Snowcap had no way—even if she had wanted to—to look up words or spellings. But Philip decided that he needed to make a stand for—standards. Without them, where would he be?

All in all, Snowcap's paper was accurate, though she did tend to wander from the subject, and about one important fact (which shall come up later), she was grievously mistaken. So Philip was perhaps harsh in ordering her to rewrite.

Snowcap thought so, at any rate. She was not known for her pleasant demeanor, and when she saw Philip's comments—*How dare he!*—she flew into a rage, ripped the paper into tiny pieces, and threw the pieces in the air. Paper rained down onto the classroom floor like hundreds of late apple blossoms, and the other students looked up from their slates in fear. Philip, in the midst of a European geography lesson, had just asked the miller's slow-witted son to name the capital of England ("Vienna," said the poor child). Now Philip turned to see what the commotion was.

"Snowcap! I say, don't destroy paper. Dear child, you know how hard it is to come by." Although brave with his red quill pen, Philip was timid when faced with actual, irate children (or their parents). He pulled his chin nervously and cowered behind his desk.

"*Rewrite??!*" screamed Snowcap, stomping on the bits of paper, her small, graceful figure twisting like a wraith. Her face blanched with anger—except the angel's kiss on her forehead, which glowed red—while her blue eyes darkened and sparked with fire. "*Rewrite??! Here's my rewrite!*" She snatched the jar of red ink from Philip's desk and dashed it straight into his surprised face. Then she pulled his lovely, clean, pressed, white linen handkerchief out of his coat pocket and smeared the ink into two lines and a half circle. Finally, she stormed out of the classroom, leaving Philip leaning against his desk, breathless and scared, his face obscured by a giant, red *R*.

Snowcap Margaret O'Kelly, Child Governor, did not rewrite.

3

STONE ROB

At her birth, Lucy had been touched by a ghost—or something even more otherworldly. Everyone (except her father) said so. As proof, she had a birthmark on her face that was the exact shape of her grandmother's hand. Everyone (even her mother) said so. The birthmark was red and covered her left cheek, all the way from her eyebrow down to her chin. Narrow, like her grandmother's hand had been (or so Lucy had been told), the mark was raised and rough and looked like a slap. Lucy's mother said a caress, but almost everyone else thought: a slap. Whenever Lucy ran her fingers over her cheek, she could feel it, scratchy like sand. It never disappeared, not even in the dark.

Lucy's father was the only person who didn't think the hand was a sign of anything. "You're not touched any more than I am," he told Lucy when she was a little girl and first overheard some older children talking about her.

"Well, but I'm ugly."

"Huh." He shook his head and glared off toward the other children, who were playing down the beach from where he was mending his nets. "You are *you*. Which makes you beautiful. Now go play."

"Don't want to."

"Hmm. Then why don't you stay and help me? You want to learn to mend nets?"

"Mending nets is for women. I want to learn to fish."

Her father laughed and held up his own mending. "You're cagey, aren't you? Want to learn a man's job?" Lucy nodded, and he smiled and looked off again toward the other children. "Now that I think of it, maybe you are marked for something special."

Later that day, they had to explain to her mother that Lucy was going to be a fisherman. Lucy's parents rarely fought, but that night as she lay on her pallet, she heard their low voices pitted against each other for a long time. They sat outside the hut, so she couldn't make out the words, until her mother cried, "But why must we raise her to be strange?" To which her father replied, "You don't see that people think she's strange already? This is what she wants. This is a good plan." The voices were quieter after that. And the next morning, Lucy began fishing with her father.

Now that her father was gone, Lucy didn't fish any-more—her mother wouldn't let her take out the boat alone—and it was just as well. After what had happened, she wasn't sure she could trust herself, either. *Maybe it's the birthmark's fault*, she sometimes thought. Maybe its curse had turned her father into a statue. Or maybe she herself had caused the turning, by what she had *not* done that day on the far beach. She should have stopped her father, or told Uncle Vale what was happening, or she should have walked out onto the beach and interrupted the meeting that had gone so badly.

Lucy's uncle Vale—her father's older brother—was in charge of all the trading with outsiders. But her father always had a plan for helping his village, or making it (as he said, in strange-sounding Anglish) more "prosperous." Unfortunately, his plans never worked out. Two years earlier he had tried to sell nets to the Anglish—but the Anglish preferred to make their own. Then he was going to organize Colay storytelling troupes to entertain in the Anglish pubs of Tathenn, but the pub owners (there were two of them) didn't want any Colay in their establishments. His newest plan was to mine lifestone and trade it to the Anglish. This plan had some merit, as he explained it to Lucy, who always listened to her father's schemes.

One morning early last fall, as they shivered in the boat together, nets down, Del had told Lucy his idea: "Lifestone is the most wonderful stone ever imagined. Born from the center of the earth"—his plans always had long introductions—"chipped from cliffs, dug from caves; sometimes smooth and deep, like pearls, with sunlight and rainbows hidden inside; and always as warm as your skin." He paused, looking almost embarrassed at such poetic talk. But Lucy nodded. It was all true. Lifestone was the most beautiful stone in the world—if you had an eye for its variety.

Del continued, picking up on Lucy's thought. "There is nothing finer than lifestone. And the pieces that are not beautiful are still useful, which is even better." He checked his net, rocking the boat so that she had to lean the other way to counterbalance. "Lifestone has a mountain of uses. Fertilizer for our crops, windows and warm inner walls for our homes, and—well, it can be molded into almost anything you want. And do you know what the best part is?" He wiggled his eyebrows at Lucy.

She pulled the net with him. "What?"

"There's no lifestone on Tathenn." They began removing fish, still flopping, into the bottom of the boat. After every few fish, Lucy rubbed her fingers to warm them. "Only here in the Colay Islands. Its power is all here. We have a what-do-they-call-it? A *monopoly*." He used the Anglish word, and Lucy repeated it after him, feeling it on her tongue, trying to make it sound as nasal and harsh as her father had.

"Actually," Del said, pausing to rub his own fingers—a sign that something big was coming—"actually, there's someone I want to meet with tomorrow. At the far beach. Can you keep a secret, Lucy-bell? We're going to discuss the future of lifestone trading. It'll be an important meeting."

"Won't Uncle Vale be there?" He not only set the terms for trade, negotiated deals, and said who could trade with whom, but Vale also spoke Anglish quite well. He was even teaching Anglish—something Lucy scorned learning, though many people in her village spoke it, at least a little—to his sons, Branch and Brady, so that they could carry on in his place when they grew up. If the meeting tomorrow were about trade, Uncle Vale would surely be there.

"No"–Del cleaned off the net meticulously–"he's a busy man. I thought I'd get this deal started first. Besides, Vale doesn't understand that our future lies in–in special trade with the Anglish. Not just trade of fish–trade of the *land*. That's where the real treasure lies. We need this kind of deal if we're going to survive."

"There are a lot of fish," said Lucy.

"For how long? Already they've got several good fishermen on Tathenn; it's only a matter of time until our fish trade is over. Anyone can fish. But we Colay have a *monopoly* on the lifestone." Again that strange word.

The next day they headed out to the far beach, the one that couldn't be seen from the village. They pulled the boat ashore long before the meeting time, and Del told Lucy, "Look for some berries, and come back when the sun is lower. I promised him it would be only me."

"Promised who?"

"The man from Tathenn. I met him last time I brought fish to trade. Now go." And he gave her a gentle shove, so that she'd know he loved her but wanted her gone.

Lucy climbed to the next hill but found no berries. It was far too late in the year for berries. A cold wind blew through her leggings and cape and whipped up her thick black hair. She stood for a few minutes, absently tracing the rough birthmark on her cheek, looking at the trees and wondering how many more days until snow fell. Then she headed back as quietly as she could. It turned out that she needn't have bothered with so much caution. The two men were talking far too intensely to notice her approach. She hid herself at the edge of the clearing, and she heard everything.

Two days later, over the course of an afternoon, her father and all the other Colay men turned to stone. *Lifestone.*

The next day Lucy stood above the sea on a cliff—the highest on the island—and threw away all her luck.

As Lucy walked through the garden holding her baby brother, she was reminded how many forms lifestone could take. She had entered the garden through the low archway of stunted apple trees. She followed the path past the statues of her twin cousins, who were holding hands, kneeling, and reaching toward the ground with their free hands as if playing mabs, a marbles game they'd loved. The twins were lusterless and white, like owls' eggs. She passed her uncle Vale and the village's head fisherman—both bumpy, jagged, and yellowed—and the priest, translucent and sharp, with a rainbow deep inside (a sure sign of good lifestone, Lucy's father had always said). Why lifestone flowered differently in different people, no one knew, but Aunt Fern's theory (she had a theory for everything) was that lifestone varied as people themselves did. At any rate, all the statues were looking weathered; lifestone was many wonderful things, but in its natural form, it wasn't strong. Some of the men and boys were beginning to crumble along the finer edges—and one of the priest's feet had snapped off. Since there was only one village on the island, she knew everyone in the garden, but in their lifestone forms, they seemed strange, unfamiliar. Way off to one side was a statue—dim, reclining, and gray—that she could not recognize at all.

Some of the statues were lying down as if sleeping, some were bent to row or pull fish, and others appeared to be sitting down to a meal. They perched or lounged, spread among the small trees and shrubs and the soft, grassy mounds of old graves from when men used to die and be buried. The earth still showed scars from where the women had carefully, laboriously dragged the statues into place eight months ago, using ropes and carts. It had taken weeks to gather them all together. In the meantime, boats darted to and from the other Colay Islands with the awful news—the same everywhere—and soon all the islands' women had built a statue garden in their old cemeteries.

Lucy passed Salter, the little boy who'd lived next door, the one who disliked her so much he ran away whenever she walked by. Disliked her or was scared of her, Lucy was never sure which. Not that it mattered anymore. Still, she paused to look at him. He was smooth and white, like her cousins, but his arms were transparent. She looked closer. Something was odd. His nose—his nose was wrong! Lucy stooped and saw a faint scar, all the way around the nose, as if it been removed and then replaced, slightly crooked. And—a little smaller, maybe. *Why?* She stood, hugging the baby to her chest and trying to think of what a crooked nose might mean, but she couldn't imagine. Then she took a deep breath, straightened her shoulders, and marched over to her father.

She looked down at the baby, and he shifted in his sleep. Then she glanced up at her father's statue.

He had been walking across a field when he turned to stone, so her father was frozen in a rather comfortable position, head up and eyes looking forward, leaning on a long staff he held in his right hand. The staff, too, had turned to lifestone, beautiful and fragile, useful for so many things—as he had told her. The Colay used crushed lifestone to strengthen the soil in their gardens; they used "soft" pieces for carving everything from toys to jewelry to bowls; they used larger translucent pieces to make windows. This particular specimen—Lucy's father—was a creamy ivory, like polished bone, silky and fibrous. Solid, good stone for carving. "Well," she whispered to the baby, "Here he is. I'll leave you with him. That won't be so lonely." Except . . . She jumped, jolting the baby awake.

Her father's left hand was gone. *Gone!* Lucy reached out to her father and ran her fingers over the broken wrist. *No, no.* As the baby cried fitfully, Lucy pawed in the weeds beneath the statue. She found the hand. Her stomach heaved and she gritted her teeth.

The baby moved into a louder register—the high, longing, ferocious cry of hunger. There was no bladder, no milk. Lucy tried to ignore the noise, but the baby worked his arm out of the blanket and waved it, screaming and screaming. As his cries grew louder, Lucy felt more frustrated than she ever had before. Her father's hand was broken. The baby was hungry. She was here, alone, far from the village. The baby might be turning to stone. *And why can't he just be quiet?*

She stood for a few minutes, willing herself not to scream. Then she cradled the baby and the broken hand together, the baby nestled in her arms with the hand resting on top like a blessing, or a weight. It was getting dark, and the moon was rising. The baby continued to cry, and she absently put her finger in his mouth again, as she'd often seen the village women do. He sucked, was quiet for a few minutes, and then began to cry again. She laid him down at her father's feet and put the hand next to him. Maybe it would comfort him somehow. In life, their father had very strong hands. Maybe his stone hand could still take care of his baby when they were both statues. She unwrapped the baby and spread the blanket around him, feeling that he should turn to stone as himself, not as a pile of blankets. He quieted, gazing wide-eyed into her face as if it were the full faraway moon.

"Ah. Hello," said Lucy softly. "Robert." It was the first time she'd said his name out loud. Then she corrected herself. "No, I think Robert is too long a name for someone so little. I'll call you Rob. My baby brother. Rob, yes? Don't cry anymore, agreed?" She patted his head gently.

Perhaps Rob approved, or perhaps it was just co-incidence, but at that moment, he reached one hand toward her face in an awkward, badly aimed baby gesture. She leaned in and his hand grazed her cheek. He kicked his legs.

Lucy did not want to leave.

She did not become soft and teary with love for Rob—she became angry. The broken hand lay like a dead beetle, its fingers curled upward. It was not her father any more than the apple trees were. She imagined the baby eventually breaking, crumbling. Never to be himself. *Tough as goats' teeth*, she thought; *our lives are that hard. It isn't fair! Why should Rob be doomed? It isn't anything he's done! Anyway, people can't just turn to stone. I don't believe it. I don't.* But deep inside she did. What else could have happened?

And still Rob reached up toward her face. She touched his left foot. Stone cold, and as pale as their father before them. She touched his ankle. Cold. His shin. Cool, growing cooler even as she touched it.

No! I won't let it happen. She leaned close to Rob's face and touched her nose to his. The empty luck pouch slid out of her shirt and dangled between them. Lucy rocked back on her heels and felt the pouch fall back on her chest. She looked into Rob's unfocused blue eyes and spoke in her sternest voice, the voice that had always terrified the little neighbor boy. "Rob, you will not turn to stone. I won't let you." Lucy grasped his left ankle. "I won't let the cold spread. It won't get past your ankle." Rob looked into Lucy's face. He opened his mouth as if to cry, but no sound came out.

Lucy had never felt so fierce. "They've cursed you." She wasn't exactly sure what she meant by that, but she kept going. "They've done it, don't you see, Rob? Or they've not cursed you, maybe. But—something. Whatever it is, you won't give in. You will not turn to stone. You will *not* turn to stone."

But anger wasn't working. His ankle felt cooler, even as she repeated the words over and over like a chant. The moon pulled itself up in the sky and the small night animals made noises all around. White-lipped, Lucy kept chanting.

Rob *did* turn to stone, slowly, as the moon rose in the sky. As Lucy held his ankle and chanted, staring into his wide baby eyes, Rob grew paler and paler. His skin shone like a pearl. His breathing slowed. His eyes glazed, dried, settled. Finally, he stopped moving altogether.

Lucy didn't know what to do. Gripping Rob's ankle even tighter, she decided to beg. "Please?" she whispered. She wasn't sure whom she was addressing, but when she looked around, the silhouettes of the statues radiated her anger and confusion. The lifestone was—was angry, too. Silently, she talked to the stones. *The baby's not yours. You know that. He's innocent. I know you're angry, and it's partly my fault, what happened. I'll try to fix it. I promise. Please just give him back to me. Please.*

After a few moments of complete stillness, while the solemn moon was at its height, Rob moved again, like a whisper.

Lucy felt a painful iciness rush into her hand, and from her hand into her whole being, but she did not let go of Rob's ankle. Her right hand stiffened and froze. The blood slowed through her arm, through her body. Her feet were two clay bricks. Her face was frostbitten, masklike. The stone curse was moving out of Rob—and into *her.*

The night passed. As slow as the moon's journey, Rob breathed again. The cracks in his skin smoothed away, and he began to turn pink and then brown—all but his foot, which remained cold and lustrous. Finally, as the moon yawned and slid down the sky, the ice in Lucy's body flowed out, receded. She tingled with a thousand thorns as, bit by bit, her body came awake and the numbness left. Only her right hand did not warm, but remained stiff and frozen. She whacked it on her father's staff to wake it up, but it wouldn't wake up. And she knew—though she wasn't sure how she knew—that

the stones had left a bit of themselves in her hand as a reminder of their anger and her promise to mend things.
With a deep breath, she gathered up both Rob and her
father's hand. Gift and promise.

Rob grew warmer. Again he was watching her, again
he moved his arms. He began to cry softly. And Lucy
loved the sound.

The moon had nearly fallen into the horizon when
Lucy realized that she and Rob were not the only people
awake in the garden. Someone was watching them. Lucy
had seen a vague, unfamiliar statue in the distance earlier
in the evening. Now, as the figure stood up and walked
toward them, she could see that it was not a statue at all,
but a woman. It was the Gray Lady.

4

LUCY FOLLOWS
THE GRAY LADY

Nobody knew much about the Gray Lady. But Lucy had heard her mother say that she was from someplace far away in the deserts of Tathenn. No one even knew her name; they all called her the Gray Lady because she now lived on the Gray Mountain. She was not actually *gray*; she was only about as old as Lucy's mother. (And though Lucy thought of her mother as very old, her mother would not have thought of herself that way, but merely as a nice, comfortable adult age.)

The Gray Lady did not talk much, and she rarely came into the village except to trade the milk from the goats she kept. Lucy had seen her only a few times.

The woman was not unfriendly—in fact, she had given Lucy's mother extra milk during her pregnancy and had mixed herbs for her that helped babies to grow—but she seemed to want to stay away from people. One day when Lucy's mother was mending a fishing net, she had brought herbs for tea. After she left, Dara said that the Gray Lady seemed sad, and that she must be missing someone.

"Why is she sad? Who is she missing?"

"I don't know, Lucy-bell."

"Then *how* do you know?"

Her mother smiled. "Sometimes you can tell just by looking in someone's face." She rubbed one hand across her large belly, looking thoughtfully at the net in her lap. Dara was very good at mending nets; it was work she had enjoyed doing with her husband in the evenings. He would return from fishing, carrying the nets over his shoulder, and after supper they would mend together as they talked over the day.

But now the family boat lay dry and empty on the shore. Before, almost all of the able-bodied men in the village had been fishermen, but now only three of the younger women carried on the task. They were all that could be spared from the children, the fields, and the goats. And none of them wanted Lucy to come along. Lucy had begged her mother to let her go alone, but her mother said it was too dangerous; she'd lost Del and she wasn't going to lose Lucy.

The Gray Lady was the only woman who did not live in the village—the outsider. "But she's not one to be scared of, Lu," Dara had told her as she picked a knot out of the net. "She's always been good to the village.

And she's been so kind to me about the baby that's coming." She loosed the first knot and moved on to another. "I wonder if maybe she lost a baby herself once." Then she had looked sharply at Lucy and put down the net. "I was thinking aloud, not saying anything that's true. Don't you go repeating these kinds of stories."

"I won't," Lucy said. "I'm not a child."

Her mother nodded and continued mending, but she didn't talk about the Gray Lady again.

Lucy remembered that the Gray Lady had come to Sunset Island a year ago, just before the so-called Rebellion. She had come in the dark of night, mysterious and quiet, and nobody knew how she had gotten to Sunset, for the Gray Lady did not own a boat or a raft. Branch and Brady, who often made up stories, whispered one day that the Gray Lady had walked across the water. Branch insisted that he had heard her splashy footsteps in his sleep one night.

"Did you see her walk across?" asked Lucy.

"No," said Branch. "I was sleeping. But I heard her, in my dream."

"If you didn't see her," said Lucy decisively, "then she didn't walk across."

"She *did* walk. I heard her, too!" Brady defended his brother, slapping the ground for emphasis.

"You did not hear her!" yelled Lucy.

And then, unfortunately, the children began fighting—pushing, punching, and kicking. Lucy's mother came out of her hut and yelled them off to the beach. The twins refused to talk to Lucy for the rest of the day. This was just as well, because Lucy would not have listened to them if they had. It wasn't that Lucy was a bad child, or a particularly unimaginative one. She simply didn't believe that a person could walk across water or do magical things. And she didn't believe she should agree with someone—when she thought that someone was wrong—just to be polite.

The next morning, Branch and Brady were still mad at Lucy, so they talked to each other only in Anglish—which Lucy couldn't understand. They even knew how to write it a little. Later that day, when the boys went to the beach, they took a piece of lifestone and wrote on the big slate rock: **NOT GIRLS**. A moment later Lucy came along. Brady helpfully translated the Anglish writing for her: "Hey! It means that you can't come over here. It means 'Stay Out.'" He spelled again on the big rock, carefully and large: **MEN**. "This one means 'Only Boys Allowed.'"

"Does not. Anyway, I don't have to obey Anglish writing."

"You don't have a choice," said Brady.

"It's written in the stone," said Branch. "You can't alter it. The stone knows."

Lucy threw rocks at them until they called her Scarface and went to play somewhere else. When they were gone, she studied the words until she memorized all of their strange shapes. She took a stick and practiced drawing the shapes in the sand until she had drawn them perfectly. Then she took a piece of lifestone and scratched out the **NOT GIRLS** until it was obliterated. **MEN** she hacked at until it chipped off in angry gray flakes. Her fingers tingled afterward, almost as if the stone understood how she felt.

Later, much later, she'd wonder if maybe her cousins

had caused something to happen by writing with the stone—into the stone. Or if she had caused something by erasing their words. Something magical and wrong. And she'd remind herself that she didn't believe in such things.

Of course, this fight had happened months and months ago, a lifetime ago, before her father met with the stranger, before her cousins turned to stone and were brought to the Lifestone Garden.

Now the Gray Lady nodded at Lucy, turned up the mountain, and beckoned her to follow.

5

SNOWCAP HAS MANY FRIENDS

After school was out, Snowcap went home for supper, hoping for an unpoisoned meal and planning to feed anything questionable to the cook. As she walked, she hummed a scrap of a song:

Treasure! Pleasure!
From India to Araby—

Snowcap remembered all the songs her mother had taught her, and sometimes when she was alone, she practiced them to make sure that she would never forget. But in public, she hummed only when she was either happy or smug. Today she was smug because she'd been powerful and clever at school, and her friends were impressed with her. The Dickens girl had said so. As they left the schoolhouse, Daisy Dickens had curtsied and simpered, "What masterful pranks in school today, Snowcap! You're so clever, and so funny. . . ." The rest of the gang nodded fervently, almost (Snowcap noted) as if afraid. She tilted her head at them—regally, she hoped—and started home feeling satisfied. Torturing Philip the Tutor was always amusing, and there had been the trick with the Gibbs girls. It was a good day . . . if she could just keep from being poisoned.

Most days were good days for Snowcap. She was clever, rich, powerful, and pretty—everyone told her so. Even the little mark above her right eye was called an angel's kiss rather than what it really was: a birthmark. She was special, and special people, she had learned, had allowances made for them. Particularly special people whose parents were dead. Particularly special people who would be Governor one day.

Of course, Snowcap missed her father and mother all the time, but she wasn't going to tell anyone about that. She'd decided that sadness was shameful and should be kept to oneself. Instead, she gathered people around her and gave them orders. When they obeyed, she was nice to them. When they declined to do her bidding, she was ruthless. People who ignored her, or who seemed not to care what she said or did, earned her strongest hatred. The two Gibbs girls, for example, thought that all they needed was each other; all day, every day, they played to-gether, sang together, dressed alike, thought alike. They seemed to truly love each other. Snowcap despised them.

Snowcap finished the song she was humming and walked on in silence. At the laundress's house, she passed under an open window and heard the woman and her little daughter talking amiably. She paused, listening.

"What happened today at school, love?" Water splashed, and clothes slapped loudly into a basket.

Lizzie recounted what Snowcap had done when told to rewrite her essay. Her mother clicked her tongue and then asked what, if anything, they'd studied?

"We learned about . . . Vienna, I think. And, oh! Snowcap dressed just like the Gibbs sisters always dress—you know, in the flowered dresses their mum makes them? She wore the same kind of hat and everything. And when I asked her if she had a new dress, she said—really loudly so everyone could hear—that she ran out of clean clothes so she had to borrow some rags from the scullery maid."

"Oh, that's not so nice for the Gibbs girls. I hope you didn't laugh."

"It was hard *not* to laugh. Snowcap was prancing around while she said it—like Bella Gibbs does, but sillier."

"Hmm."

"It really wasn't funny, though. Snowcap is very pretty, Mama, and clever, but she's . . . hard. Like ice, or stone. I don't think she has a heart."

"Child! Hush. Someone might hear you. Hand me that basket, please. Anyway, how could you say that about anyone? Everyone has a heart."

"I don't know, Mama. Maybe some people have too much other stuff inside, and the heart kind of squishes out and—lands on the floor."

"What a picture that makes in my head!" They laughed. "Now hang these for me, love. I've got to change the baby's clothes."

Snowcap continued home, deep in thought. The next day, she came to school with her hair in fat braids, just like the laundress's daughter.

6

Tutor, Embezzler, and Artist

For as long as he could remember, Philip had wanted to be a writer. And not just any writer, but a Famous Author. He had developed an elaborate and beautiful signature befitting an artist:

(He did indeed autograph his name this way, for the dramatic flair of the extra *P*.) He had a fine, bold signature.

Now he needed only to write the books.

When he began his first job as a bank clerk in Nottingham, Philip found it didn't leave him much leisure to pursue his writing career. He did, however, find time to practice his autograph.

When he was caught, tried, convicted, and sentenced to be shipped off to America for embezzling bank funds, he feared that his dream was over. (For the record, he was guilty.) He was still a young man, just the right age to commence being a Famous Author, but indentured servants in Virginia were not, he had heard, allowed much time to pursue the literary arts.

Yet Philip never gave up. *Somehow* he would write. For example, he could write an exposé of prisoners' lives in Virginia, or a guidebook to the flora and fauna of the land. Or he could even write a story of his own criminal life and his remorse and repentance in the New World. (While in prison awaiting transport, he had read a book by a convict named Moll Flanders who had been shipped to America; why shouldn't his vigorous story be even more popular than this woman's flimsy tale?)

But the shipwreck had been the final blow. How could he publish a book while marooned on an island? How could he begin living the life of a Famous Author? Impossible. For the first few years, all of the English—including Philip—were busy building houses, clearing land, planting crops, setting up new laws, and negotiating with the Colay, the native Tathenlanders. They were too busy to read—or write—books.

But after the town was settled and life seemed to be running smoothly, Philip began to dream of writing again. *Perhaps it is possible*, he thought. He stopped the Governor on the street one day and announced that he wanted to be an author.

The Governor laughed. "How would we print your writings? And who would want to read them? There are only twelve of us convicts who can read whole sentences. Philip, you're a plum." Governor Robert O'Kelly slapped Philip on the back and walked away.

Philip hadn't slept all night, but spent his time pacing the floor of his room, thinking about what Shakespeare would have done in his place, deserted on such an island and surrounded by people who didn't understand his genius. He decided he would write an essay on this very problem, entitled "Shakespeare's Son." But Philip couldn't think of enough to say, and he didn't have any paper to write on, so long before morning, he gave up on writing his first essay.

Three days later, the Governor stopped Philip on the street and said, "Philip, old boy, I've been thinking about your idea."

"You want me to write something?" Philip asked, his hopes rising.

"No, not exactly." The Governor coughed. "You see, we don't really need a writer in Baytown just yet. But we *do* need a schoolmaster—a tutor. We've been here a little while, and we have young squirts now—children, my boy! Why, my little Snowcap is eight years old, almost old enough to start learning things. If they are going to be strong rulers, our children need a sound English ed-u-ca-tion! And you, yourself, are an educated man. . . ."

The Governor smiled. Philip, dismayed, did not.

"So," Governor O'Kelly said, "you think on this offer. Head Tutor of the entire island, responsible for all our children!" The Governor coughed again, delicately. "And—it may give you some time off to write. We would get hold of bark-paper and ink, as much as you need."

Philip took the job.

But, surprisingly, he did not write.

Many things distracted him from his plan of being a Famous Author. First of all: his students. Philip found that he had to study and create lectures to keep ahead of them. Then, more recently: the O'Kellys' deaths. Philip was unable to write in the face of tragedy. And now: he was stuck. Every day he thought up new and brilliant ideas for masterpieces, but he had not the slimmest idea how to start writing or which of his brilliant ideas to write first. He was disgusted with himself, and he could not write when he was disgusted. This depressed him, and he could not write when he was depressed.

He gave himself a stern lecture: *You cannot become a Famous Author unless you actually sit down and write.*

So, one sunny afternoon (in fact, the very next day after Snowcap inked his face, the day after Lucy carried Rob to the statue garden), Philip set himself the task of writing something, anything, before he went home. For an hour he sat at his desk and looked across the schoolroom, out the window to the bay. The time was right; a muse of some kind was surely hovering nearby. He would begin to write today.

But what should he write? History? Biography? Legends? Science? Poetry? Well, he would try his hand at them all, one by one. Then he would decide which one was his calling. He had to be a genius at something.

He began that afternoon—with a map.

7

A Map: Of Tathenland

With his very best curly penmanship, Philip drew and labeled a map. Then he was moved to begin an essay.

Perhaps, he wrote, *you are right now looking at an atlas, trying to find Tathenland. I would not be surprised if the country did not appear on any European maps. It is a newly discovered territory, a former <u>terra incognita</u>, which we have claimed for England.*

The enclosed sketch of Tathenland is based upon descriptions by several explorers, including the first Governor and his wife. (I myself have never journeyed to the western and southern parts of the island.)

I can tell you without a doubt that the main island of Tathenland—Tathenn—is roundish and perhaps about fifty miles in diameter, much smaller than England. Still, Tathenn is so much bigger than the little Colay Islands to its north that the Colay people must think of it as their mainland—the way that the Irish must think of England as <u>their</u> mainland. The thirteen tiny Colay Islands form two strings, which, from the heavens, might look like two strands of green-grey pearls floating in the ocean. The Colay Islands are not important, however. The natives herd and fish there, but the land is too rocky to be valuable for anything else. It is all stone. Tathenn, on the other hand, has rich land for planting crops, plentiful fishing grounds, and perhaps even deposits of gold in the deserts to the west.

Philip stopped writing. He was stuck as usual. First of all, he was making up the part about the gold. In addition, he didn't know Tathenn well enough to draw a detailed map, and he had never visited the Colay Islands. He wasn't certain of the exact size or location of any of the islands, much less their shapes and landmarks. More importantly, he couldn't think of anything else to say about Tathenland. There was nothing, in his opinion, special about this land—except that it had been discovered by the English. Lastly, it appeared to him upon consideration that it was nearly impossible to write about a place without first telling the history of the place.

He needed to write a history.

The Atlantic Ocean
(N.N.E of Virginia)

The Colay Islands

Naked Mountain and Cliff of Good Hope

Botanist's Bay (Bay of Oddities)

Baytown (Pile)

Sunset

The Forest

The Desert

Plantations

The Island of Tathenn

N

Tathenland, 1787

8

In Which We Meet Adam and Learn Once Again How Snowcap Treats Her Critics

Snowcap left school that afternoon again feeling smug. Because of the previous day's ink-in-the-face incident, Philip the Tutor was still ignoring her, so she'd had a lot of time to sulk, tease the laundress's daughter with her silly fat braids, and spit grape seeds at the dressmaker's two perfect little girls. A very good spitter, Snowcap aimed at the backs of their heads and the grape seeds stuck in their hair. This final activity is what put her in a better mood. And what a sap Philip was! He hadn't even tried to punish her, not for any of it—*proof*, she thought, *that he is afraid of me. Good!*

Because her other option was to go home and watch

Sir Markham and his steward, Renard, pretend to like her while trying to poison her, she went—as she often did—straight to the stables, only a few minutes' walk beyond the house. Adam, the groom, was there, picking burrs out of Robberbaron's mane as the other horses grazed nearby. As Snowcap approached, her horse, Peat, broke away from the group and galloped up to her, whinnying. She hugged his neck.

"Good day, kid?" Adam asked. He was the grown-up nearest to Snowcap's age; only eight when he'd been transported, he was now twenty. She sometimes thought that when she was old enough, she would consent to marry him. Not that he had asked, but surely he was just waiting until she was older to broach the subject. Or maybe he was afraid to ask, since he belonged to a class so much lower than hers. Well, there was no one better around, so she'd condescend. Besides, Adam was very handsome with his thick, brown, wavy hair tied back with a string, and his broad chest and long, strong legs. He would make a good escort to balls. Except—

"Can you dance?" she asked.

"What? 'Course. Oh—you mean like at some nib ball? No, never studied that in my gentlemen's college." He disentangled a small burr from Robberbaron's mane.

It didn't matter. There was time for him to learn before she was grown up. Next summer, when she was thirteen, she'd suggest dancing lessons.

"Any reason for askin'?"

"Not yet." She twirled around. "Want to hear what happened yesterday?" Snowcap told Adam how Philip had criticized her writing. "How dare he. I'm the Governor!"

"Not Governor *yet*."

"Near enough."

Adam shrugged and took a knife out of his work bucket. "Now that's like saying a princess is same as a queen. Or a ragamuffin same as the king of the gypsies." He separated Robberbaron's mane to cut out a particularly large and entangled burr; the horse neighed but stood still. "If you spell poorly, shouldn't the Tutor catch you at it?"

"Oh, what do you know? You can't even read."

Adam paused to look at her, raising one eyebrow.

"And don't tell me what to do!" She kicked lightly at the ground.

Adam pursed his mouth, turned back to cutting out the burr, then asked, "Wha'd you do to Philip?"

"Ooh, that's the best part! I threw ink on him! And he didn't punish me at all! He didn't do anything today, either—I think he's scared of me. Isn't that funny?" She stretched out her arms, patting Peat's neck absentmindedly. "Think of all the things I can do, now that I know this!"

Adam frowned. "Wouldn't it be better to be the kind of folk that others ain't afraid of?"

Snowcap rolled her eyes. "Not if you're the ruler of a country, you dolt! Or the future ruler," she added.

"Snowcap,"—Adam flicked the burr on the ground—"your old man was a rum Governor, and he didn't have to blast terror in people's hearts to do it." Adam spoke with quiet intensity. "And he wasn't rude," he said, turning away.

In one flowing move, Snowcap swung onto Peat's back and looked down at Adam. She felt powerful—and angry. *More criticism! How dare he! How dare anyone!* She stuck out her chin. "I don't need to listen to the likes of you," she said. "A grown man, and all you are is the horse boy! You're just—a thief. From a family of thieves. None better than the gallows you'll hang on." She watched with pleasure as Adam reddened, stiffened, and finally walked away to lead Robberbaron out for a run. *As if he's good enough to marry a Governor! Ha!* She galloped away.

9

The First Page of Philip's History

Drawing a map, thought Philip, *is not the same as writing. It is just—a map. No, geography will get me nowhere.* He pushed the map aside and stared at his new, empty page. What kind of history to write? He would never admit this to his students, but although he was a wonderful speller, he had a lot of trouble remembering dates and names.

He decided to start with something small, something simple—a history of Tathenland. And since it would be the first history of its kind, no one would know if he happened to get a fact or two wrong.

A Brief History of the English in Tathenland
By Philip Tudor

A group of brave English explorers, 137 men and their 99 female consorts, valiantly settled the island of Tathenn in the year 1775. They claimed the land as a colony of England and set up a model government, the first Governor being the stately Robert O'Kelly, the youngest offspring of a prominent member of the Irish gentry. The English landed at Tathenn with three ships, all of which had been damaged in a fierce storm. They built a proud and happy colony in which agriculture, commerce, and especially the arts flourished. . . .

Philip's history of the convicts' travels to Tathenland was not entirely accurate (nor was his name, as he was unrelated to England's royal Tudor family). English records stored in London will show that three ships—the *Restoration*, the *Memory*, and the *Hopewell*—embarked together just over twelve years earlier, in April 1775, for the Virginia colony in America, carrying, altogether, a load of dry goods, several dozen good sets of silverware (originally destined for a Richmond belle's wedding), twenty-one horses, 255 convicts, and sundry crew members. The convicts were to be sold into indentured servitude in Virginia, and after seven years, if they were lucky, they'd be set free to make their fortunes in the New World. But Providence had another plan, for the three ships disappeared en route to America, and the ships' owners supposed that they had gone down in a storm. The crew, convicts, and horses were presumed dead.

The convicts—who survived to become the English colonists of Tathenn—still talked about that fateful storm. This is one version of the story they told:

The three ships were caught in a terrible weeklong gale and blown off course, far to the north (though how far north, no one knew for certain). When the ships began to list and take on water, the crews clambered into their lifeboats and deserted the convicts, who were chained in the holds of the ships.

The convicts felt their hearts collectively sink. They were forsaken! Some began to cry. Many were sick. The boats rocked horribly and leaked freely. In the *Restoration*, a hysterical man named Philip screamed, "We're going to die!" over and over, until the scurvyish young forger and magician chained next to him (named Renard) punched him with a handcuff and mercifully knocked him unconscious. (Philip awoke later, after all the fuss, with a piercing headache and the sense of having missed something exciting.)

In the *Hopewell*, a young Irish woman well into her pregnancy (who was soon to become Snowcap's mother) took the hand of her husband next to her and then reached across him to take the hand of an eight-year-old boy. "You know that I love you, Robert," she said to the big man, in Gaelic. Then in English she spoke to the boy: "Adam, you've become like a younger brother to me. I want you to know . . ." She began to sob softly.

Robert smiled and kissed her hand, but he showed no sign of fear. He spoke in strongly accented English: "See, I've been waiting until the right time—and now must be the right time."

"The right time for what?" asked the boy. He was looking toward the deck hatch as if he expected Someone in Charge to open it, descend the ladder, quiet the crowd, and say calmly, "It was only a false alarm. You're all right." But no one did.

"My chains are loose. With your help, I can pull them out," said the big man. "Nora, you pull on one, and Adam will pull the other." Robert strained and strained, bulging his neck and shoulders, as his partners pulled. And after a few long minutes, the chains began to slide. Groaning, the pins squeezed themselves slowly out of the wood block into which they had been screwed.

Robert kissed Nora, patted her round belly, and whispered in Gaelic, "Thanks, love." He thumped the boy's shoulder and said, "Nora is right. You are a little brother to us." He stood for the first time since the storm began and grinned, swiveling his hips to loosen his joints. "Wait here. I'll be back soon." People up and down the hold immediately began to call to him. Waving, he shouted, "One moment, fellas!" and ran up, out of the hold, to the now-empty captain's cabin. There he searched until he found a set of keys. He returned to the hold and began to free his fellow prisoners.

As Robert freed them, the winds died down and the waves calmed. Dragging their weak bodies onto the deck, the convicts saw, by the light of the slow, gray dawn, that they had weathered the storm. The other two ships flanked the *Hopewell*, leaking as badly as she was. But wait—land was nearby! The three ships floated, nestled in the small harbor of a large island or perhaps a mainland. A string of smaller islands lay behind them; the ships must have drifted past them in the last hours of the storm. And then the convicts saw before them on the shore: a half circle of small but sturdy boats and a dozen dark-skinned men holding fishnets, amazement on their faces.

The brave Robert O'Kelly, a petty thief from Ireland by way of London, waved and shouted, "Hullo, gang!" The fishermen consulted together but did not wave back. After a brief discussion, several broke from the group and headed inland; the others climbed into their fishing boats and rowed out to the *Hopewell*, where they picked up the convicts and ferried them ashore. The first convict to set his feet on dry ground was a young man named Mark the Ham, who despite the long voyage remained inexplicably clean, neat, and well fed. (Adam's theory, unproven, was that he had bribed some of the crew for bathing water and extra food.)

After the fishermen emptied the *Hopewell* of its swamped inhabitants, they began to empty the *Restoration* and the *Memory*. Robert O'Kelly entered both ships first and, with young Adam assisting him, set the prisoners free and helped them up on deck. The fishermen managed to retrieve all the horses as well—quite a trick, really, and almost worthy of another story—and most of the silver and dry goods. Then, finally, the ships gave their last groans and sank.

The islanders who had disappeared inland now returned. They brought more men and women and carried large bowls of bread and stew. They appeared happy to greet and help the newcomers. The prisoners, dazed and weak, were relieved simply to be alive.

The ships' crews were never seen again.

10

The Curse on the Colay

When she saw Lucy carrying the broken hand of the statue—in her arms, cradled next to Rob—the Gray Lady asked for it and tucked it into her cloak. Lucy didn't inquire what she planned to do with the jagged stone. She was glad to be relieved of it.

Following the Gray Lady, Lucy carried Rob out the back of the garden and up a small, winding path. The sun was almost up, and the sky was brightening; Lucy could see the trail clearly and could hear the nighttime creatures making their last noises before settling down to sleep. Lucy and the Gray Lady walked up the mountain until they came to her hut. It was the first time Lucy had seen it. Except for its color, glowing faintly as the sun rose, the hut was nothing special. It looked much like the huts in the village, made of clay and straw, with a thatched roof. But the clay had somehow been dyed or painted a bright yellow, the color of sunshine.

Lucy followed the Gray Lady inside and looked around. The hut was the same size and shape as her mother's, with the same irregular mud brick walls—but it seemed warmer, cheerier. It was yellow inside as well as out. In its roundish single room, rush mats covered the floor, straw and a blanket were spread along the back wall to make a sleeping pallet, and two tiny goats—not much larger than Rob—snuggled in the middle of the floor. Several jars and a large cooking bowl were neatly stacked near the doorway. The house was cozy, not like a warm bed on a dark night, but like a sunny field in summer. Light streamed in through the large east window, which was made from the biggest and clearest piece of lifestone that Lucy had ever seen. Plants curled over the windowsill, spreading tendrils out to the light. Drying herbs hung from hooks in the ceiling and swung in the light breeze from the doorway.

"Sit down," said the Gray Lady, motioning to the straw mattress. "You must be tired and cold. It's hard work to watch a sick child all night." Lucy sat in the warm patch of sunlight on the mattress. She was suddenly very sleepy, too sleepy to speak or ask questions. Her right hand, the one that had been frozen, now ached and burned as if just thawing from frostbite.

The Lady reached in the folds of her cloak and removed the stone hand and a broken stone foot—the priest's, Lucy realized—and laid them down gently on a corner shelf. "You may be wondering how I found you. You see, I was very interested in the fate of the last baby on Sunset. But"—she knelt next to Lucy—"sleep first." She reached to take Rob out of Lucy's arms.

"No! He's mine." Lucy yanked him closer. She hadn't meant to snap, but she was so tired.

The Gray Lady shook her head. "I was watching children long before you were born. I'll watch him until you wake. We'll stay right near you."

Lucy felt herself frowning and heard herself say "no" again, but Rob was pried from her arms as she slid down, down, down into a blanket of sunlight.

When she opened her eyes, Rob was wrapped in a clean blanket and lying at the foot of the bed, awake but not crying. Lucy sat up and stared into his face. He didn't have the wrinkled, worried look that most newborns have when they first meet the world; he looked solemn—the world was a serious thing, but he was not afraid. He stared into Lucy's face as if he recognized her. Lucy knew it wasn't possible, yet he *did* look as if he understood how things were.

The Gray Lady was sitting cross-legged in the doorway, facing out and stirring something into a pot. When Lucy picked up Rob, the Lady turned to them. "I hope you've had a good sleep. I made us some porridge."

"Is it already afternoon?" Lucy asked, looking toward the small west window. Narrow shafts of light were streaming in and landing on the rush mats on the floor.

"You were tired. But let's talk while we eat. You need to decide what to do with your brother."

They sat in the doorway of the hut, Rob quiet and

alert in Lucy's lap. Lucy was very hungry. She started on her porridge, but then put down her spoon.

"He was—turning into a statue."

"Yes."

"But then he turned back."

"Do you know why?"

"No."

"Will you take him home?" asked the Gray Lady.

Would she? Surely he couldn't go back to the village? The women thought he was cursed; even her mother thought so. And maybe he was.

"No," Lucy said. "I don't think he can go back home. Besides, they don't want him. Or me." *And for that, they don't deserve him,* she thought. *Or me.* She began eating again.

"Hmm," said the Gray Lady. "You never know these things for certain. They might be happy to see him."

"They threw him away."

"Sometimes people do things they later regret. Mothers, too."

"Not me. I never regret." Lucy leaned forward, and her hair fell over her marked cheek.

"That's really too bad." The Gray Lady brushed her hand across the baby's forehead. "So, not back to the village. Then where?"

Where? Lucy looked around the hut. "Can he stay here with you?"

"If the village is dangerous for him, then I imagine the mountain is also. They both share the same small piece of land."

"Then maybe I need to get him off the island."

"Where would you take him?"

Lucy could hear curiosity and concern in the Gray Lady's voice. *Where indeed?* She had nowhere to go; she knew no one who could take the baby. "I don't know. I think the other islands would be the same. And I don't know anyone on Tathenn. I've never been there." Lucy remembered her father's promise to take her to the city of Picle (or, as the Anglish called it, Baytown). "You can help me with the lifestone trade," he had said. "Learn Anglish, count money, barter. You have a good noggin for it; I can tell. My practical daughter." And he had rubbed the top of her head fondly. But there never was a trip to Picle.

Now the Gray Lady asked, "Would you like to go to Tathenn?"

Lucy shrugged.

The Lady reached out and took hold of Lucy's chin. She studied her face, lingering on the crimson hand-print. Lucy glared back. She pulled her chin away. "What are you going to do with that stone foot and my fa—and the hand?"

"I'm going to fix them."

"How?"

"I heat them down to powder. Then I add water and reshape them on their statues, and when they dry, they become a new hand, a new foot."

"Did you do Salter's nose?"

"Poor child. It was my first effort. I'm getting better each time."

Lucy muttered, almost but not quite under her breath, "I hope so."

"You know," said the Gray Lady, "lifestone is the only rock that you can turn to powder and then back to stone. The only one that can be reborn that way."

"Fascinating."

The Gray Lady narrowed her eyes. "Perhaps we should change the subject, since you don't seem interested in this one. Why don't you tell me something: how did the men turn into statues in the first place?"

Lucy jerked and smacked her head against the doorway. "Why do you think I would know?"

"You know something. You have that look about you."

"Well, I don't . . . know anything."

"Now *that* is fascinating. Why don't I tell you a story, and then you can tell me a story?"

Lucy sighed. "Thank you for all your help," she said. "But I think I should be going now."

"Where?" the woman asked sharply. "My story *is* important, though you may not realize it yet. It's the story of these islands, of us and the Anglish."

Lucy felt a bite of curiosity. "And the–the Colay Rebellion?"

"As I'm sure you know, the Colay did *not* lead a rebellion." The Gray Lady spread out her arms on her lap, palms up. "The Governor and his wife had one child, on whom the sun and moon shone down. They raised her to be smart and strong, and they raised her to be kind."

"Kindness is overvalued."

"Interesting. That's exactly what the Governor's daughter might say today. But as I was saying: There was another man, greedy for a title that was not his, and he arranged to have the Governor and his wife killed. It was made to look like the Colay were the guilty party–"

"Did he do that? Make us look guilty?"

"I'm not sure if he did it or if it was someone else, but at any rate—"

"What does this man look like?"

"Child, haven't you been taught that it's rude to interrupt a story?" The Gray Lady impatiently flipped her hair down her back; it was a thick blue-black—mingled with gray, of course—and cascaded from its knot like a dark waterfall. "Well, this greedy man is tall and thin, with a sharp brown beard. Not a strong man in body, or mind, but in desire—very strong. His name is Mark the Ham, often called Sir Markham now. *Sir* is an important title to the Anglish."

"He has a beard? Then he's not—" She stopped.

"Not what?"

"Nothing."

The Gray Lady waited, but when Lucy didn't elaborate, she continued. "Mark the Ham is the Protector of Picle and Anglish Tathenn. Ruler until the Child Governor comes of age."

"Even if he killed the first Governor?" Lucy gave a short whistle. "I'd be awfully mad if I were that Child Governor."

"If I were that Child Governor, I'd be afraid," said the Gray Lady.

They sat for a few minutes in silence, Lucy leaning against the doorway of the hut and Rob asleep in her lap. The Gray Lady finished her porridge. She rubbed her mouth slowly with her fingers. Then her eyes narrowed in on Lucy again, not unfriendly, but piercing nonetheless. "Whom did your father meet with?"

Lucy took a deep breath. "How did you know?"

"I saw two boats at the south beach one day. One of

them was your father's. The other was Anglish. Then—two days later—you know what happened. But tell me—were you at that meeting?"

"My father sent me away."

"But you were there?"

Lucy frowned.

"What happened?"

So Lucy told about Del's plan. "He was only think-ing of the good of the village."

"Only?" The Gray Lady raised her eyebrows. "Who else was at the meeting?"

"I don't know his name. A small Anglish man, beard-less. Bent. Like claws. Like—a heron. So, not your person, not Markham. They talked about trading lifestone, and he threatened my father—"

The Gray Lady held up her hand. "Take a minute to think it over, and then tell it like a story, so I can see it, too. I'll try to keep from interrupting," she added dryly.

11

OF GYPSY-UM AND LIFESTONE

As Lucy told it, this is the story of what happened on the south beach that day:

When she returned from her walk and she saw her father and the Anglish stranger, she hid behind bushes. The Anglish man was talking, in accented but clear Colay: "We call it gypsy-um." He smiled down at the translucent stone in his hands, turning it over and over, his shoulders hunched toward the rock as if to protect it. "You've made quite a find for us—something that will improve our life on Tathenn. It's not a wonderful stone—it's not gold. But it's useful."

"Gypsy-um," said Lucy's father. "That's a lovely name. What does it mean?"

"It means a rock," the Anglish man said. "It means gypsy-um." He tossed the rock lightly in his hand. "Now show me where it is."

"Where it is?"

"Yes." The Anglish man waited, but Del did not respond. "Surely you don't expect me to return to Tathenn with just one rock? I need to see it all. I'll be sending men to mine it."

"No—I mean—that's not what I meant—"

"Did you think you'd just show it to me and let me drool over it, and then tell me that I can't have it?" The Anglish man laughed, but not in a friendly way.

"No. . . . We Colay will dig it up, and we'll bring it over to Tathenn to trade." Del smiled broadly and clasped his hands together. "For embroidered cloth and glue and metal pots and . . . whatnot." He trailed off.

"Oh, I see." The Anglish man's voice became even more nasal and sharp. "You want to lord it over us. No, that won't happen. You tell me where the gypsy-um is, and I'll collect it."

Del unclasped his hands. "No. No. I'm sorry to have wasted your time. I thought we could make a deal. But now I see that I'll have to talk with someone else, someone who can be more . . . reasonable."

The Anglish man gripped the stone as if he were about to throw it. "*I* am the man you deal with." Then he did throw the rock, overhand and fast, at a tall oak tree. A squirrel dropped to the ground. It lay unmoving in the dirt. Del stepped back, and the man smiled coldly. "Think of me as—a magician." He used the strange Anglish word, then translated to Colay. "A shaman. I know how to change men into something more valuable than men."

"What do you mean?"

"I mean," the stranger grated, "I wanted the gypsy-um, and it could have made me rich. I don't *need* it, however. In fact, you've given me an idea for an even better plan. So—you keep it. And"—he waved his hands—"may you be up to your ears in it. But know this: You think you can make deals? You think you're in charge? Hubris!" (Another strange Anglish word, incomprehensible to Lucy.) His right hand closed again, as if gripping another stone. Then he pulled back his arm and threw, fingers stretched stiffly toward Del's chest. In her hiding spot, Lucy felt a sudden chill; it looked as if darkness streamed from the stranger's fingers. He continued: "The Anglish own all the land here. *Me*." Fingers still outstretched toward Del, his voice cold and hard. "You have nothing. You *are* nothing."

Del took another step back, as if he'd been pushed. "The Governor won't let you—or the Protector—"

"The *Child Governor*? And her *Protector*?" The Anglish man laughed, throwing his head back and straightening his spine so that he looked, for the first time, taller than Del. "The titles mean nothing." He walked over to the oak tree and scooped up the rock with one hand and the dead squirrel with the other. "But I'm sure you know all about wanting power, or you wouldn't be here trying to trade with me, *fisherman*." He tossed the squirrel at Del's feet. "Here's a little something for your supper. Be sure to share it with the entire village—since they'll be sharing your bad luck as well." He got in his boat and pulled away from shore, rowing vigorously despite his hunched form.

Del watched the Anglish man leave. Then he buried

the squirrel beneath its tree and went down and sat in his boat, still beached. Lucy waited a few more minutes before she came out of the bushes.

"How did it go?" she asked quietly.

Del watched the waves intently. "We'd better get in some fishing before we're expected home." They headed out, and after a few minutes of steady rowing, he said, "I just wanted what was ours, Lucy. Not a thing outrageous about that." He didn't talk again for the rest of the afternoon.

Lucy stood up. "Now you know. It was our fault. *Mine*, for not telling what I saw."

"Untrue," said the Gray Lady. "Not yours, and only partly your father's. But I'm glad to hear the story. It helps to explain some things."

Lucy walked away from the hut, stood under a tall oak, and looked up; several squirrels were fighting, or maybe playing. It was hard to tell with squirrels. The story she'd just told was one she wouldn't have understood if she hadn't seen it for herself. Even so, she wasn't sure she understood it all. She paced back and sat on the ground outside the doorway. "What—what do you think happened?"

"It sounds like this man is indeed something like a shaman," said the Gray Lady. "It sounds like he's meddling with the powers of the land."

"Maybe he's just a magician," said Lucy, testing the Anglish word.

"Maybe. But we still don't know how to fix what he's done."

"*Is* there any way to fix it?"

The Gray Lady stood up and stretched. "The land always fixes itself. Eventually."

She walked into the hut, so Lucy raised her voice. "Have you heard that there is a prophecy that someone might remove the curse?"

The Gray Lady returned with a small pot of tea. "You've heard of the desert philosophers?"

"Yes. They live on Tathenn, far to the west." Lucy took a long drink and shuddered. The tea was bitter and tasted of dandelions.

"They have prophets among them. They sent me here with one, a young man named Beno." The Gray Lady paused over the name as if caressing it. "We arrived before the men turned to stone. Beno visited all of the thirteen islands. The devastation was terrible: every man and boy frozen wherever they were, whatever they were doing."

"Beno didn't turn to stone?"

"No. But he might have, if he had stayed here. He went back to the desert. Before he left, he did what he could."

"What did he do?" Lucy remembered the men and boys turning to statues quite clearly. But she had no memory of Beno. Perhaps he, like the Gray Lady, had come in the dark of night and stayed hidden in the mountains.

"He suggested the statue gardens. He thought that bringing the statues together would make the tragedy easier to bear. And, in a way, it has."

"What about my brother? And the prophecy?"

"Beno did one other thing to help the Colay: he could not change the fact of the curse, but he countered it with words of his own. He prophesied that someday a child born of the Colay—on Sunset—would save the people." She turned to Rob, still sleeping in Lucy's arms. "This child is the last one born."

"So he *must* be the one!"

"So he *might* be the one. Prophecies are possibilities, no more and no less. And they don't always work as we think they should."

The Gray Lady whistled a long, low musical whistle that hovered between two tones. Presently three goats ran up the trail, one with a bunch of clover poking out of its mouth. They were full-grown goats, much bigger than the two kids that huddled in the hut; they were nearly up to Lucy's waist. She was tempted to cuddle them.

"Hello, little ones." The Gray Lady knelt and petted the goats. "Lucy, meet my good friends. Roseroot is the one with the mouthful of clover. Sunshine is butting you. And this is little Cattail." She patted the head of the smallest goat. "They gave your brother milk—while you were sleeping."

"Oh," said Lucy. She felt ashamed. Rob had awakened but was so quiet now that she had forgotten he needed food even more than she did.

The Gray Lady milked the three goats into a bowl, which she poured into a little bladder. "I had to nurse Cattail when she lost her mother," she explained. "Now the bladder comes in handy again." She handed it to Lucy. "Why don't you try to feed the baby now?"

Lucy laid Rob in her lap. She dribbled a little milk into his mouth, and he began to drink immediately. Lucy still felt stiff and tired from her night in the statue garden. She thought about how easy it could be to stay here. But if she stayed simply because she didn't want to go, she would be a coward; and whatever else she might be, Lucy wasn't a coward.

She needed some advice. "I don't know where to take him."

"It is a problem. The desert seems the safest place. The Anglish don't go to the desert."

"Why not?"

"It's not useful land. It is a good place to be a philosopher, but a bad place to build a city and set about farming. And it's a hard place to get to. Because of the wild pups. Careful, you're spilling."

Lucy wiped Rob's face with the edge of his blanket and dripped the milk into his mouth more carefully. "Wild pups? I thought they were just a story."

"Just because they're a story doesn't mean they're not real. And as mean as you've heard. They're not even as tall as your knee, but they travel in packs, jump high and run fast, and bite with teeth like razors. And they live in the woods you must travel through to reach the desert."

"Then how can I get there?" Lucy asked, exasperated.

"By boat—hug the coast until you pass the woods. You'll probably see the pups on the shore—you'll surely hear them out hunting, night and day—but if you're lucky, you won't have to deal with them. Remember that they can't climb trees, and they don't like fire or water."

Lucy nodded, and the Gray Lady continued, telling how the wild pups came to inhabit Tathenn. It seemed nothing ever just happened; everything had a story. Just as Lucy was wondering if the history of the pups would ever end, the Lady finished, briskly moving on. "I'll give you more milk before you leave, changing rags and blankets, and a pot and food for you, too. But you'll run out of milk, so I'll show you another way to make food for the baby. You won't meet with many goats in the forest." She paused. "What do you think?"

Lucy didn't allow herself to mull it over. "I'll go. How long will the trip take?"

"I don't know. It could take a week to reach the desert. Then a few more days to reach the philosophers. I'll draw you a map before you leave. But—I have one more story to tell before you go."

"*Another* story?" Lucy rolled her eyes.

The Gray Lady stared straight through her, and Lucy quailed. "Of course," Lucy said in the most gracious tone she could manage. "Another story."

12

LEAVING SUNSET

As she spoke, the Gray Lady brought out a length of net and began to mend it, the leisure work of all the Colay Islanders. She worked with quickness and precision, tying the knots, running her fingers along each string, and pulling the web tight. Lucy marveled, as she often did with her mother, that anyone could make such a difficult and time-consuming task look easy and graceful. Making a net, though interesting to watch, was essentially the same act every time; but mending was always new. The net never tore exactly the same way twice.

The Gray Lady told about the original people, how they rose out of the sea and rock to found the Colay

Islands and the island of Tathenn. Lucy had heard versions of the myth many times, especially during the winter around the fire. But the Gray Lady was a good storyteller, and Lucy started listening in spite of herself, noting the Lady's gestures, repetitions, and inflections. As she listened, she rocked and burped Rob, who fell asleep, a look of calm satisfaction on his face.

Upon finishing her tale, the Gray Lady sat in silence as if waiting for Lucy to respond. Then she said, "Child, do you realize that stories are treasures? You must guard them carefully. Don't give them away without thought; tell them only at the correct time."

Lucy nodded sullenly. She hated being made to feel stupid, and she hated when people talked mysteriously. What in the sun's name did the Gray Lady mean? Lucy knew that some stories were told only at certain times of the year, and that certain stories were bedtime stories, while others were more daytime stories. But why should she *guard* a story? And how could you know when the time was right to tell it?

The Gray Lady wasn't put off by Lucy's scowl. "History is in the mouths of the people who tell it. Everyone believes the lies about the Colay because those lies are the official story of what happened. Do you see? Whoever tells the story controls it. Whoever knows the story of their own past possesses something as important as—as children." She glanced at Rob, and Lucy pulled him closer. "Children are like prophecies. More important, actually."

"You're a prophet, too, aren't you?" Lucy suddenly felt she needed to know.

The Gray Lady smiled. "Yes, I'm a kind of prophet. But not in the way that you think of the word. I simply remember old stories and retell them."

Lucy was crestfallen. For a moment, she had hoped for a prophecy—something that would tell her that she was doing the right thing.

"What we could use now," the Lady said slowly, "is a shaman. Not like your Anglish man. A *real* shaman—one who can commune with the land and find out what's wrong."

"You mean someone who can work magic and fix it all?"

"No," said the Lady, looking disappointed. "Not like that."

Lucy wasn't sure what she'd said wrong. "Is there a shaman in the desert?"

"They're rare. The Colay haven't had one for several generations now." She searched Lucy's face, looking for an answer to an unspoken question. "You'll leave tonight," she concluded, holding out her arms for the baby. "Until then, you should rest."

Lucy gave her the baby, went inside the hut, and lay down, snuggling her aching hand under the blanket to warm it. She slept.

Lucy dreamed a wonderful dream: that Rob was dressed in soft, clean deep-blue robes and that all the people of Tathenland (Anglish and Colay) were bowing to him—though he was still a baby. She woke certain that he was indeed the baby meant to save her people. That he would defeat the curse. Maybe he would even become a shaman. And she alone would make this possible, by getting him away from the islands until he was strong enough to return and conquer.

Opening her eyes, Lucy saw that it was almost dusk. The Gray Lady was feeding Rob from the bladder. "Just in time for supper. Help yourself, child."

Lucy walked the short steps to the bowls sitting at the doorway: dried fish and early greens, cooked together until warm and soupy. She sat down and quickly began to eat.

"I thought you should have one more hot meal before you left. That is, if you still intend to go."

"Bore than ebber," said Lucy. She swallowed the mouthful and tried again. "More than ever. I've figured it all out. I have to save him—"

"You may take my boat." With a thin stick, the Gray Lady drew a map in the dirt. "Go to the shore west of Picle; it's too dangerous to stop in town. Stay close to the shore—but avoid the pups—and paddle west until you come to the big bay, the Bay of Oddities; the Anglish call it Botanist's Bay. I don't recommend swimming or fishing there." Lucy was about to ask why, but the Gray Lady continued. "If the weather's fine, you can paddle across the bay and save a bit of time. After the bay, keep heading west. When you see the trees thin, and you no longer hear the pups, you can beach the boat and walk southeast. Carry water with you. You'll reach the desert soon, and after another day, you will reach the hills. Look for three long hills clumped near an oasis; there you will find the desert philosophers. But don't worry too much about finding them. Chances are they will find you."

Lucy finished her meal in silence, studying the map and reviewing the directions in her head: avoid the pups, avoid Picle, don't swim in the bay, head west by boat and then southeast by foot. She felt confident she could do it. Of course she could! Maybe two weeks, at most,

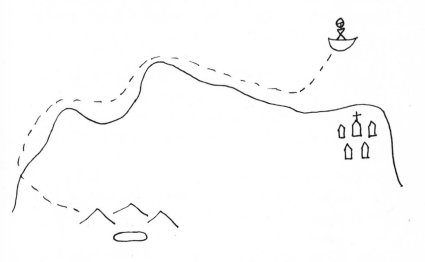

and then she would be back home with her mother in Sunset. And Rob would be safe. They could stay in the desert for as long as they needed; they weren't wanted at home, anyway.

Oh! How could she have forgotten? Her mother must be worried beyond measure. She'd never returned from the statue garden yesterday! She choked on her stew and stood up, coughing.

"Dara is fine," said the Gray Lady, as if Lucy had spoken. "I went to her last night, while you were still in the garden with the baby. I said that you were upset and would stay with me for a few days. I'll see her again tomorrow and tell her where you've gone and why."

Lucy sat down, relieved. "How did you know to tell her that? Back then, I mean?" *And how had the Gray Lady traveled so fast?*

"Well, you were upset, were you not? Let me show you how to make food for the baby out of these walnuts. You mash them, like this, and boil them. See? It's not ideal, but it'll do in a pinch."

Later, when night had settled on the mountain and Lucy was ready to go, she cleaned Rob's changing cloths one more time, trying to use her right hand as little as possible. The Gray Lady watched. "Does your hand bother you?"

"I'm fine," said Lucy.

"Ah. Well, I might have suggested keeping the hand wrapped up. *If* it bothered you." She paused as Lucy lifted Rob back into her arms. "Dara told me his name is Robert."

"It's such a big name for a baby. I call him Rob."

The Gray Lady smiled. "That's appropriate." She patted Rob. "Now you will steal away with him." She bound Rob to Lucy's back with a long strip of cloth. Then they walked down the mountainside to a tiny private bay where she kept her boat. Lucy grinned to herself. *Wait until I tell Branch and Brady that she doesn't walk on water*—and then she remembered that she couldn't tell them anything.

The boat was a canoe made of a large hollowed trunk lined with tar, only as wide as a single person but longer than a tall man. They tied Lucy's supplies in the front in a knapsack; Lucy would sit at the back to paddle and steer.

The Lady rubbed the inside of the canoe with her palm proudly. "I finished making this only last week. I thought it might be of use."

Then there was an awkward silence as they both hesitated to say good-bye. Lucy shrugged. The Gray Lady said, "If you find you need help as you travel—"

"I won't. I can do it myself."

"Yes, but—if you do need help, don't be afraid to ask. There may be some who will help you, befriend you."

"I don't need friends."

"You might change your mind."

"I don't—"

"You might. A person can change, Lucy. Even you." She raised one hand, palm out. "May the sun shine on your journey. And tell Beno hello from Amarrah."

"Who?"

"Me," she said dryly. "My name is Amarrah."

"Oh. I thought—I mean—I didn't know."

"You never asked. Please tell Beno I hope to see him again soon."

"I will," Lucy said. She wanted to go, but she was not sure how to leave, and she shifted from foot to foot.

The Gray Lady (*Amarrah*, Lucy reminded herself) stepped forward and reached as if to caress Lucy's face, but Lucy shrank away, and the woman's hand dropped. "Go well." She kissed Rob's forehead. (He was, once again, asleep.) "Go safely."

"Stay well." Lucy completed the formal good-bye. "And thank you. And—good-bye." She turned and got in the boat, a little clumsily with the extra weight of the baby.

Then Lucy paddled away, never looking back at the Lady or the island, though she knew in her heart that they were both watching her until she disappeared into the dark.

13

In Which Snowcap
Eavesdrops and Learns
Some Unhappy News

Sir Markham had the nasty habit of pressing his fingertips together as if he were thinking of choking someone. He was not only tall and thin, but also almost completely bald, his only hair of substance being his small bodkin-beard that looked sharp enough to slice bread. Snowcap thought his smile looked hungry. Sir Markham always gave Snowcap whatever she wanted, and whenever she threw temper tantrums, he would smile broadly and say, "What a dear child!" or "What fine spirit!" But Snowcap knew that he didn't mean it.

She could tell from his horrible hungry smile that he didn't like her, and she didn't like him, either.

But worse than Sir Markham was his steward, Renard. He was a kind of secretary and butler and jack-of-all-trades, and he was small and cruel. He was also smart—one of the few English who could read and write (he had taught himself)—and crafty. Full of tricks and sleights of hand. Snowcap suspected that most of the decisions Sir Markham made were suggested by Renard. Sir Markham was not a shining intellectual light.

Snowcap watched these two closely, mostly when they didn't know she was around, and was both impressed and frightened by how easily Renard seemed to manipulate Sir Markham. Snowcap's mother had seen a puppet show once at a fair in London and had told Snowcap all about it: how the man held the strings from above so carefully, how he made the little wooden dolls dance and say funny things. Watching Renard with Sir Markham, Snowcap felt as if she were watching a puppeteer at work.

Except for the horses (especially Peat) and the groom, Adam, Snowcap didn't like anyone who lived on her estate. (They felt the same way about her.) But the two people she hated the most were Sir Markham and Renard. Renard had once been a famous young forger (and magician) in London. When he spoke to Snowcap he was always snide, curling his lip and correcting her grammar. Though he was always hunched over, his spine like the top of an *f,* Snowcap was not fooled into thinking he was weak.

And, of course, she was also certain that Sir Markham and Renard were trying to kill her.

So when Snowcap came home after her argument with Adam and saw Sir Markham and Renard scurrying down a hallway (the very same afternoon that Lucy was getting ready to paddle the Gray Lady's canoe to Tathenn), she decided to follow them. Snowcap had a gift for prowling; she slipped along like a shadow. Yet the men stopped frequently and peered around before hurrying onward.

When they reached the cellar, the two paused to light a lamp, and Snowcap crept along the wall and hid behind a cider barrel. She peeked around the barrel and watched: they were bent over a table beneath the hanging vegetables and dried herbs. The lamplight played grotesquely over their elongated faces, casting huge silhouettes of their heads on the ceiling, surrounded by wavery shadows of onions and carrots.

Sir Markham pressed his fingers together. In a low voice he whined, "I am tired of waiting, Renard. I want to be king."

"And you *will* be. But there are some small matters to be taken care of first."

"Small matters. The child, you mean. But she refused her breakfast. Our plan isn't working. *Your* plan. A failure."

Renard curled his lip so high it threatened to envelop his nose, but his voice was as slippery as melting ice. "Then it's time to change plans, don't you agree?" He paused delicately. "Perhaps . . . a kidnapping?"

"A kidnapping," Sir Markham mused. "That might work."

"And we might blame the Colay again. That's better than poison."

Sir Markham gazed at the hanging vegetables, forming some kind of thought.

Renard leaned toward him. "We kill her but frame the Colay. It'll be even *easier* than last time—people will naturally believe us. Nobody likes her to begin with. And it's the only sure way to get what you need. What this *country* needs."

Snowcap, still crouched behind the cider barrel, was almost indignant enough to leap up and scratch their eyes out. But, in spite of her fury, she knew that she would learn more—and stay safer—if she remained hidden. Still, she was incensed. In addition, she was confused: What did they mean by "last time"? Were the Colay innocent? Had they *not* killed her parents, after all? Then . . . ?

Renard continued, his hand moving rhythmically back and forth in the air as if he were directing slow music. He paused with the beats. "It's *time*, sir. We've waited *long enough*. No one will suspect *us*. It's a *good plan*."

"A good plan."

Renard leaned back, his head in shadows. "Mar—Sir Markham, you are a genius. Your people will truly appreciate your rule, your Highness."

"Don't call me that. Not yet." Sir Markham shook himself as if he'd just woken up from an unplanned nap, and began to crack his knuckles, one after the other. It sounded to Snowcap like corks popping out of wine casks—the way the Great Room had sounded just after she'd been proclaimed Child Governor a year ago. The day after her parents' deaths, when her life changed forever. Corks popping sounded like death now, like Sir

Markham coming to her in the garden and telling her about the "terrible accident, a tragedy really," like the end of love.

"Now, to the details," said Sir Markham, after the last knuckle pop. "We'll nab her next week sometime—"

"Why not tonight?"

"Oh. Yes. We'll nab her late tonight and—and drop her into the oubliette."

Renard moved back into the light, but his face was still unreadable, streaked with shadows from a string of carrots. "A perfect plan. Then we'll announce all around town that she's been kidnapped. After a few days, we'll pull her up from the pit, dead, and show what the Colay have done to her."

"Yes, yes!"

"We should have a ransom note, hmm? In case anyone needs to be convinced she's really been kidnapped?"

"You may write one, dear Renard, from the Colay. Make it clear they are trying to gain power once again. I hope your skills are in top form."

"What a delightful challenge! And—as you know—since they can't write, it'll have to be done in pictures. I wonder if we could take care of another problem at the same time: Adam."

Sir Markham gazed again at the ceiling and rubbed his chin. "Adam is still suspicious, I think. Of the O'Kellys' deaths."

"That he is. He has some sort of attachment to the girl as well."

Sir Markham grinned, his beard stretching into a curved blade. "Well, he can't *like* her. Nonetheless, he could be a problem. Perhaps . . ."

Renard waited, but Sir Markham did not continue. Finally, Renard said, as if the thought were only just occurring to him, "Perhaps when we find poor little Snowcap, killed by her Colay nabbers, we could find her in the stable. Then we would realize that Adam is in cahoots with the Colay."

"Oh! Brilliant."

Renard cleared his throat. "Milord, you are truly a genius." He bent low over Sir Markham's hand.

Sir Markham bestowed a beatific smile upon Renard and touched the top of his head with a regal flick of his wrist. "And for your kindness and heroism in helping me uncover this plot, you will be generously rewarded. Do remember that."

"I will. Is there anything else, milord? Would you like me, perhaps, to dig up some reliable witnesses as well?"

"Certainly. If you've got the time, you may find a few English or Colay to testify against Adam. But we'll use them only if needed. The ransom note is the most important thing. Don't fail me." He snapped his fingers. "Oh—you might include a short, pathetic note from Snowcap herself, to verify that she is indeed held by the Colay. I'll give you a sample of her handwriting—some old school papers that nitwit Philip gave me to show me her 'progress.'"

"He gives a bad name to thievery, that fumbling jarkman. We could also—"

"No," said Sir Markham firmly. "We have enough on our plate right now." Renard bowed again.

The men left the cellar, carrying their lamp. Snowcap slunk after them, silently battling emotions. Mostly, she felt—as she often did—angry. How dare they try to kill her? But part of her also felt sad and confused. *Did* Adam dislike her? *Would* everyone believe she'd been kidnapped? Most important, *what* had happened to her parents? And *how* exactly were Sir Markham and Renard involved?

She straightened her shoulders. Answers could wait. Now she had to take action. She ran quietly upstairs and during dinner, which she ate very carefully, she planned out her strategy.

Eavesdropping is also a nasty habit, but it was a good thing for Snowcap that she didn't care. She still had time to disappear before they killed her.

14

PHILIP'S HISTORY OF
THE REBELLION

As Snowcap sneaked around the Governor's mansion
listening to plans of murder, Philip sat in his empty
schoolroom and continued his history, skimming through
the initial good relations between the English and the
Colay and moving quickly to the conflicts, which culmi-
nated in the Terrible Rebellion (the deaths of Nora and
Robert O'Kelly) and its successful Bloodless Quashing.

*The people called the Colay transpired to murder the
Governor. They killed him and his lovely wife, Nora, while
the trusting pair was out alone, horseback riding, and then
endeavored to make it seem as though the horses had*

thrown them when startled by a rock slide. But several English persons grew suspicious (especially the loyal horse groom, Adam). These persons convinced the Protector, Sir Markham, to look into the mysterious deaths. Sir Markham's steward, Renard, investigated and immediately found that the dastardly Colay people were guilty of the murders, as part of an unsuccessful coup attempt. In his great wisdom, Sir Markham banned all Colay Island men from living on the entire mainland of Tathenn. The men retreated to the centres of their northern islands, and to this day—except for brief trading visits, which have ceased in recent months—they have not dared to venture on Tathenn again.

The inaccuracies in Philip's account were not wholly his fault. He simply didn't know that the Colay were innocent of any coup attempt. But the inaccuracies were at least partly his fault, because he didn't *want* to know that the Colay were innocent. The Rebellion story was questionable on several points (Why did Sir Markham wait to investigate? And how did Renard find out the Colay people's guilt so quickly?), but Philip did not try to solve these problems or verify the story. He wanted to believe, because it felt safe and comfortable to blame the Colay. And he retold the story—even though it was, at best, insipid palaver, and mostly a pack of lies from start to finish.

15

RUNAWAY

Snowcap ran away that very night. She really had
no choice. She knew that the people of Baytown didn't
like her, and she thought it possible—likely, even—that no
one would believe her if she claimed that Sir Markham
and Renard were plotting her demise. After everyone in
the house was asleep, she packed a change of clothes and
a rope into her bedroll and sneaked downstairs. (She
wasn't sure what she would need the rope for, but it
seemed like the sort of thing one packed when running
away.) As she stole into the larder to grab a knife and a
knapsack of food, she reviewed the past week, trying to
see herself as the residents of Baytown might see her.

Snowcap had never attempted to look at her actions from someone else's perspective before, and it came as a surprise to see just how mean she had been. Why, within the last week alone she had been exquisitely and forcefully nasty to quite a few people:

1. **The Gibbs girls and the laundress's daughter.** And a few others at school, mostly girls, who would not flatter her and do her bidding.
2. **The cook.** Because the cook had forgotten to salt her bread pudding, Snowcap had tossed salt all over the kitchen floor.
3. **The gardener.** She had plucked his favorite daisies to wear in her hair to school.
4. **The horse groom.** Snowcap remembered the fight with Adam from that afternoon and felt a bit queasy.
5. **The tutor.** In addition to the Red-Ink-in-the-Face incident, he had, earlier in the week, suffered through the Red-Nosed geography lesson. Philip had unwisely corrected Snowcap. "My dear child," he said timidly, "China is not a colony but a—um—a continent." Snowcap ran at him and tweaked his nose so hard it was red the rest of the day. More than one person he passed on the way home wondered if tutoring the Child Governor had finally led him to drink.
6. **Two women at the market.** They had clucked at her when she pushed to the front of the queue to get an apple, so she elbowed them both in the stomach on the way back, while eating the apple.
7. **Four small children at the docks.** The little monsters had thrown a ball in front of Snowcap and Peat

when they were out for a walk. Snowcap hopped down, picked up the ball, hopped back onto Peat, rode to the end of the dock, and threw the ball far into the bay while the children yelped and scattered.

8. **Many government ministers.** Snowcap didn't know the exact number, but at the start of the week she had insulted all of them by storming out of the annual House of Commons dinner, knocking trays of hors d'oeuvres out of the waiters' hands and shouting, "You're all imbeciles, and when I am Governor, I shall hang every one of you!" (This she did for no reason whatsoever, except that she was in a bad mood, and she had been longing to use the word "imbecile" after having recently learned it, in passing, from Renard.)

The past week had not been exceptional; each and every week consisted of Snowcap berating and insulting the citizens of Baytown. Now, as she considered where she could run, Snowcap realized what a liability her mean-ness might be. She didn't feel sorry for all the horrible things she had done, but she did see that acting hateful toward the entire populace of Tathenland hadn't been a very wise idea. She regretted—for purely selfish reasons—letting her hot temper guide her actions. She had nowhere to go.

However, there would be time for more reflection later. How she wanted to take Peat with her! But he was so big and easy to spot—he wouldn't be able to hide in small corners like she could. When she had found a safe place for him to stay, she would come back for him.

Still, it was an effort to leave Peat behind. She dared

not even say good-bye, in case he whinnied too loudly. She picked up her bedroll and her knapsack of food, slipped out the pantry window, and pinned a note for Adam—who couldn't read—on the door of the stable. She had thought about the note long and carefully and finally sketched a picture of herself running away. Then she drew Adam—standing next to a horse so that he'd be sure to know it was him—to urge him to run away, too. She didn't know how to draw treachery and being framed, but she wanted to make sure that Adam knew he needed to escape.

Then Snowcap eased over the low wall into the main garden; wound her way down its intricate and well-ordered path; and scaled the high wall in the back, throwing her packs over first and climbing after them. She paused for a moment at the top of the wall, and her almost-white hair caught and thickened the glow of the moonlight. She pulled her dark hood closer, eclipsing the radiance; lowered herself over the other side; and disappeared into the alleys of Baytown.

Snowcap knew her way around; Baytown was not large—more of a village—and she had lived there all her life. She had rarely ventured outside its boundaries, and then only for a day at a time, to have a picnic or to accompany her parents on an inspection of the surrounding plantations—and she hadn't left at all since her parents died. She therefore knew very little geography outside of Baytown. She knew that the plantations were to the south and east, the sea was immediately to the north, and the woods—her only hope of hiding and escape—were to the west. Cautiously, she wound her way through the narrow, twisty streets, stopping once to slip a note addressed to Philip under the baker's front door. (The baker couldn't read, but his son was one of Philip's smarter pupils. And Snowcap knew their family would be up before dawn and would surely deliver the note early. Philip, himself, lived on the east side of town, as far from the woods as possible.) She pressed into shadows, scurried down alleys, and slid along walls and around corners. Few people were out so late at night, and those few neither saw nor heard her.

When she reached the western edge of Baytown, Snowcap hesitated. Unlike the other borders, which were open and friendly, the western boundary was marked by a wall more intimidating than the one around her garden. High and broad, stone piled upon stone, this wall had been there when the English landed; the Colay had built it long ago to keep the woods from encroaching on their village of Picle. But then the English came, and their Baytown sprang up and eventually crowded out Picle, advancing all the way to Picle's old village wall, where it halted for the time being.

Snowcap had seen the West Wall all her life; she had been within a handbreadth of it many times. But she had never done what she was contemplating now. The forest was a terrifying place, and although the English claimed that they would take it over and tame it one day, they had not yet accomplished this task; they had not even begun. When Snowcap was a little girl, an English man would occasionally take it in his head to live in the forest. He would gather supplies, walk into the woods with his hatchet slung over his shoulder . . . and disappear forever. This happened three times before Snowcap's father passed a rule forbidding people to enter the forest except on official government business.

Snowcap wasn't afraid of breaking her father's law—after all, she was in charge now, or would be when she turned fifteen—but she was wary of what the woods held. People who had been there said vicious animals roamed the forest. Even Adam, who had traveled through the outskirts of the woods, said he'd heard wild dogs barking. There were stories of giant rats that swarmed in packs and gnawed travelers to death while they slept. Snowcap knew that these tales (like many stories) might be somewhat exaggerated, but she also firmly believed that they were founded on nuggets of truth.

She had no direction to turn, however, but west. The sea would lead only to the unfriendly Colay; in the plantations, she would be immediately recognized and returned. She did not waste time hoping that some kindhearted soul would believe her story and try to help her. She was smart enough to realize that people wouldn't be likely to put themselves in danger for her.

There was nowhere to go but up, over the wall, and into the woods. Whatever lay ahead.

It's not very surprising that Snowcap became lost almost immediately upon entering the forest. She had never traveled in deep woods before—she rarely traveled by foot anywhere, preferring to ride Peat—and, through the trees, the moon provided barely a glimmer to see by. She slowly walked farther and farther in, trying not to leave a trail behind her.

Snowcap traveled most of the night, determined to walk until she became too tired to continue. In reality, she became disoriented. Unknowingly, she spent most of the night wandering, not in circles exactly, but in winding switchback paths that took her to the edge of a stream, very near the sea, and not more than a mile west of Baytown.

At this stream she stopped, exhausted. Dawn was beginning to seep through the leaves and drip down to the floor of the forest. Snowcap needed to sleep, but she was afraid to sleep in the open, unprotected. She had not heard any sounds all night long–which in itself was scary, especially when she *knew* that animals were out there, somewhere–but now she suddenly heard a high-pitched howl, far away, followed by faint, high yappings. *Rats? Dogs?* Snowcap didn't want to find out. She peered through the darkness for a safe spot and, looking up, saw she was standing beneath a huge beech tree.

The beech was wide and its bark lumpy and bunched at the base of the trunk; it looked as if the tree's stockings had slid down to its ankles. Low branches–low enough for Snowcap to reach if she jumped–swung out over the stream. And higher up, several large branches reached out, all from the same point, like the fingers of a fat hand. Snowcap smiled. It wouldn't be the most comfortable of beds, but as weary as she was, it looked good. She could scrunch up her blanket to make a little nest, and she could use her rope to tie herself to the branches so that she wouldn't fall in her sleep.

And that is what she did. Snowcap was asleep before day broke open, and as the sun rose she slept on, curled in the palm of the tree.

16

RENEGADES

By the light of the pale moon, Lucy—still carrying Rob on her back—paddled the canoe to Tathenn and neared shore just west of Picle, where the woods began. Amarrah hadn't said where to sleep. Lucy didn't want anyone to see her, neither the residents of Picle (she refused to call it Baytown) nor any of the women from the islands who might be out fishing or gathering seaweed tomorrow. So she decided to hide in the woods during the day, at least until she was farther away from Picle and the Colay Islands. She'd follow Amarrah's directions again at nightfall.

After paddling along the shore for an hour, Lucy

found what she was seeking: a river. It was actually more of a stream, not wide nor deep, but substantial enough to hold the canoe. Lucy paddled up the stream into the woods. She didn't go far, because she was very tired and the woods were immediately thick enough to hide the canoe from anyone more than a few feet away. After first listening carefully for wild pups and hearing nothing, she went ashore—*my first steps on Tathenn!* she thought. Without her father.

She unwrapped Rob from her back. He was awake but, thankfully, quiet. She fed him and changed him, rinsing out his dirty cloth in the water and draping it over the front of the boat to dry. He seemed content, almost as if he knew that he was being taken to a safe place. Lucy rewrapped him snugly and placed him on her cloak in the bottom of the boat.

Then she noticed the stone in the bottom of the canoe: a piece of lifestone white and faultless, the size of a baby's fist, so smooth and perfectly egg shaped that she wondered if Amarrah had carved it. *But why would she do that?* Still, it was beautiful. Lucy reached out her hand. The stone was warm to the touch. She held it against her cheek and felt a comfort like flowing water. When she put it down, she found she missed it. So after piling branches in the front of the canoe, she picked up the stone again and, for safekeeping, slipped it into her empty luck pouch.

Then she tied a rope to one of the canoe's cross-beams and climbed back in. She pushed the canoe to the middle of the stream, grabbed the low overhanging branch of a fat and sturdy beech tree, and tied the boat securely to it. This done, she stretched, tucked away her paddle, covered the canoe with the branches to disguise it from anyone (or anything) that might happen by, and curled up in the bottom of the boat.

"You see?" she said softly as she settled on the rough brown cloak next to Rob. "Look how far I've taken you already. We'll get all the way there. By ourselves." She yawned. "Without help." She shifted to ease her sore shoulders. "Oh," she murmured, "I'm so tired." And she fell asleep, one hand on Rob and the other holding her new stone in its pouch.

The beech tree above her rustled in the late-night breeze. Lucy woke once, peered up through her green nest, saw nothing and heard—what? *Only a squirrel climbing up a tree*, she decided. And she fell back asleep.

Slow and bright, morning filtered through the thick trees, and the sound of wild pups yipping far in the distance faded away. It was going to be a good summer day.

Girls and baby slept.

17

PHILIP DETECTS A FORGERY

The note that Snowcap slid under the baker's door was found by the baker's wife very, very early the next morning. It was secured inside a larger, folded sheet that Snowcap had addressed to the baker's son:

> Petr, plese give this note to Philip the tooter.
> Thank you, Snowcap.
> P.S. Do nott read it. It is privotte.

But since Peter did not know what "privotte" meant, of course he read it—and truthfully, he probably would have anyway. So when he delivered the note to Philip (he actually went to the classroom an hour before lessons started to make sure that Snowcap could have no reason to fault his delivery service), he already knew its contents: Snowcap was ill and would not be in school that day. Or, as the note stated:

Snowcap is sik and wil not be at lessons today.
Plese exquse her.
Signed Sir MarkHam

Philip knew the letter was a forgery. Snowcap could no more imitate Sir Markham's flowing script than she could his spelling. Well, he'd go over there at noontime and find out why she was ditching her lessons and forging notes to excuse herself. Or maybe he'd wait and go over *after* lessons; it would be nice to have a quiet, Snowcap-free day. He smiled at the thought.

Distractedly, he thanked Peter and excused him. Then he turned his mind to the task at hand, for which he had arrived at school an hour early himself: to write something wonderful. He began.

18

THE LIFE OF PHILIP TUDOR OF TATHENN [A FRAGMENT]

Following numerous requests from friends and acquaintances to immortalize myself in print, I, Philip Tudor of Tathenn, record in the following pages my humble life for posterity. May my tale be useful in teaching moral and upright living and especially in guiding youth on the proper path.

I was born the youngest son of the influential Lord Parsons of Nottinghamshire. The commoners called me "Robin Parsons," because like my namesake Robin Hood, I stole from the rich to give to the poor, breaking English law for the noblest of purposes. I even went beyond Robin Hood, who gave the poor <u>material</u> help only. I gave them spiritual help as well: I wrote poems, songs, and essays to inspire the *hungry masses. I was a young Artist. Alas, the law is blind, for I was arrested for thievery in 1774, at the age of twenty-three. The judges, moved by my benevolent actions as well as my flowery rhetoric, pardoned me and sent me to America as a correspondent. I was to accompany a ship of convicts and write about them, describing their experiences in the New World.*

I became friends with the nobler of the convicts as we travelled, especially the brave Robert O'Kelly, once a general in his majesty's army, wrongfully convicted of robbery. It was he who gave me my new name, Philip Tudor, to denote my royal bearing. Soon, all the better sorts of convicts called me by this name.

Upon our arrival—in Tathenland—

Here the document broke off. Philip couldn't quite figure out how to account for his life in Tathenland. He didn't know how to explain his becoming a schoolmaster or—more to the point—his *not* becoming, well, someone important. What had gone wrong?

It was just as well that Philip stopped writing his life story, as it was not quite true in every particular. Philip *was* from Nottinghamshire, but after this point, fact diverged from fiction. Had he been telling the whole truth, it would have looked something like this:

Philip Parsons, the youngest son of a poor, minor baronet, grew up in Nottinghamshire, where he was generally thought of as a snitch with sticky fingers. He had very few playmates. As the youngest son, he stood to inherit nothing but his father's oldest horse, a brass candelabra, and a small collection of Latin texts. His father didn't even have enough fortune to purchase Philip a commission in the army (not that he wanted one). Philip would have to find a paying job. More than anything, Philip wanted to be an Author. That is, he didn't want to write as much as he wanted to be thought of as One Who Writes—a man whom people invited to parties, a man with bedroom eyes and unruly hair, a man who didn't have to hold a paying job.

He didn't write much—because he was too busy *thinking* about writing—and what he did write, no one wanted to read. One morning, his father cleared his throat over his tea and said, "My dear boy, I will no longer support you. Martha, more tea, please. And another biscuit."

That was that. Philip knew he had no choice. But he didn't know how to look for a job. He mostly sat, quill in hand, and hummed to himself an old tune that his mother had taught him:

You are the treasure I long to find;
I ask for you everywhere.
I search all ships setting out to sea;
I search all the birds of the air.

And whether you are near or far,
And whether we're green or gray,
I'll seek you, find you, and bring you home
To live in my heart always.

Philip could not explain what he wanted, but he knew it wasn't a job. He wanted something . . . more. The song seemed to know, so he sang and waited for his fortune to arrive.

Philip's brother-in-law helped him get a position as a lowly bank clerk.

As a still-aspiring Author, Philip began to practice his handwriting, especially his autograph. One day, he saw a way to make money with this skill. Soon he was writing signatures (other than his own, that is) and embezzling large sums of money. When caught, he became known as "Robbing Parsons," the bank clerk thief. The trial was short; under English law, he was sentenced to death.

Once again, Philip's brother-in-law helped out. As a justice of the peace, he managed to get Philip's death sentence altered to exile: Philip would be transported, as an indentured servant, to America. After seven years—doing whatever nonpaying job his master told him to do—he would be free.

Philip sailed for America in the ship *Restoration*, in company with the *Memory* and the *Hopewell*, in April of 1775—along with 254 other convicts. Nineteen prisoners died en route, one of old age and the others of gaol fever and the Influenza. All the others—236, including Philip—survived, but they were destined never to see the shores of Virginia. They arrived at Tathenland, and the rest, as they say, is history.

19

THE NAMES OF THINGS

Lucy woke with a start. Somewhere far above the canoe, the sun was shining brightly, but here in the forest, thin bands of light quivered and blinked on the shaded creek. Dragonflies and mosquitos—as large as dragonflies but, fortunately, fat and slow—buzzed lazily. Rob was whimpering with hunger.

Lucy fed and changed him, talking to him all the while. When women on Sunset talked to their babies, Lucy had always thought them silly, but now, talking to Rob felt right. He couldn't possibly understand the words, yet he *seemed* to. He must have liked the tone of her voice for he quieted down. Lucy told him his story, how he was the baby who would save the Colay. "You will be the one who will stop the curse. When you return to Sunset. When you are a little older." Her voice carried into the trees.

Lucy laid the sleeping baby gently in the bottom of the boat and once again washed his changing rags in the stream. She tied the milk bladder to the boat and lowered it back into the water to keep it cool. Sometime today, she'd have to start boiling and mashing the nuts so that Rob would have enough food. It would slow them down, but it couldn't be helped. Besides, they weren't in any hurry. She was doing fine with their travel, following all of Amarrah's instructions. Most of them, anyway.

She ate some food herself and then stripped off her clothes. A quick swim would ease her shoulders. She waded into the stream, which was only waist high at its deepest point. Had it been deeper, this wouldn't have posed a problem, for Lucy had learned to swim almost as soon as she'd learned to walk, in the often icy waters around Sunset.

The sun reached the stream, but only barely. Still, Lucy thought, even faint light was better than the darkness of the night before. She trusted day more than night. Things in daylight were, well, more *real*. Looking around from the middle of the stream, she was amazed to remember that last night, she had *almost* thought she heard someone cough near the boat. Last night, the stream looked wider and darker; last night, the trees looked heavier, united and menacing. But now, in daylight, she could see that the trees weren't trying to fool her by casting large shadows or by disappearing into the gloom. They were simply *there*, like the stream and the rocks and the shrubs. Daylight, Lucy decided, had less mystery than night: it was more honest.

She waded back to shore, shook herself off, and put her clothes back on her damp body. Then she heard a noise from above.

It sounded like a laugh—a nasty laugh. She looked up and saw a foot, a smallish human foot, dangling from a low branch of the beech tree. Attached to that foot was an Anglish girl, wearing a black, flowing hooded cape and smiling in an unpleasant way that matched her laugh.

"Hullo," said the girl. "Fancy meeting a little Colay runaway here—with her brother, the mighty savior of the Colay." She spoke Colay with an Anglish accent, but understandable. Lucy frowned and then, startled, realized: *She was listening!*

"Yes, I heard your little story," the girl continued. "People like you and me should be traveling together." She tossed her head. "Do you know who I am?"

"No," Lucy said. "And I don't want to travel with you." She stuck out her chest. "I was just telling a story. It's not really true. It was just a story to make the baby quiet."

"We'll see," said the nasty girl. She swung down from the beech tree and alighted on the ground, weightless as a bird, a graceful feat Lucy could never have accomplished. Except for her deathly pale skin, this was a girl that Bastia would have called pretty. Lucy decided she did not like this girl at all.

The Anglish girl stood straight and gave an impression of great height, though she was really shorter than Lucy and much skinnier. "Do you know who I am?" she repeated. She spoke loudly and slowly. "I'm Snowcap Margaret O'Kelly." She paused, but Lucy did not react. "The Child Governor." She tossed back the hood of her velvety cape to reveal her shocking white-blond hair. On her feet she wore sturdy Anglish-style boots, and over her shoulder she had coiled a length of rope. Nothing she wore indicated she was the Child Governor. Though Lucy had never met any Anglish children, she had heard that the Child Governor wore boots and had pale hair and a bad temper. However, Lucy had heard the same about many Anglish children: according to Branch and Brady, who had traveled once to Picle, all Anglish were fair-haired, bad-tempered, and oddly dressed. Her appearance proved that this girl was Anglish but *not* that she was the Child Governor.

She's playing tricks to see how dumb I am, Lucy thought. "Well, Governor, I'm the queen of the Colay," she said.

Snowcap's face turned red, and she stamped her foot. "I *am* the Child Governor!"

"Huh. Then what are you doing *here*?"

Snowcap sighed as if making a painful decision. Then she spoke rapidly, leaning toward Lucy so that her cape swirled dramatically around her shoulders. "I've run away from my home. You must help me escape to freedom." She smiled encouragingly now—because she wanted something.

Lucy turned her back to Snowcap, crouched down, and began to repack her food.

"What are you doing?" Snowcap asked sharply. "You can't leave. You have to help me. Sit down, and we'll make a plan."

"No," said Lucy, not turning or sitting. "I have my own plan. I'm bringing the baby to—to his aunt to raise. We don't have time for a nasty, foolish child who wants to pretend—"

Snowcap grabbed her arm and hissed, "You'll listen to me if I say you will. *And* you'll help me. I'm the Child Governor! And besides"—she looked slyly at the boat where Rob lay sleeping—"I know people who would be interested to hear your story. And if I went home tonight and let it slip, and they came to find you . . ."

Lucy looked up at her. She could be punished as a rebel against the Anglish for what she had said. And Rob would surely be killed if the Anglish shaman found out about him: he wasn't supposed to come to Tathenn; he was supposed to be a statue. This stupid girl could get them both killed, and the Colay people would never be saved! Lucy felt dizzy. She wouldn't have admitted it to anyone, least of all to this horrible creature, but she was scared.

Snowcap shrugged. "You see, I like to tell stories, too. But I'm sure you won't mind. After all, you'll soon be at your—aunt's, is it?"

Lucy willed herself to move. She rose and shook her arm out of Snowcap's grasp. Very well—she would do what she had to do to save Rob, even if it meant playing this simpleton game. She tightened her mouth grimly and sat down on the grass. "What do you want?"

Snowcap laughed and clapped her hands together. "I knew you would see my point of view!" She dropped down cross-legged, facing Lucy, who refused to look at her. "All I need is some help to rescue Peat, my horse. Then you'll tell me how to get to the desert. This philosopher place you talked about sounds like a safe spot to take Peat."

"Where is this . . . horse?"

"Baytown."

"You want me to go to Picle?" She couldn't, certainly not with Rob. "You're crazy."

Snowcap stopped smiling. "You *will* go to Baytown and help me rescue Peat, or I will turn you in. Don't worry—you and your precious baby won't get caught."

This girl must be the Child Governor, Lucy thought. *Who else would be this cruel?* Then she noticed—and spoke before thinking: "You have a mark on your face." No one had ever mentioned that the Child Governor had a birthmark.

"What? Oh—it's a beauty mark." Snowcap touched the little pink spot on her forehead, above her right eye. "Called an Angel's Kiss." Snowcap used the English word for *angel*, because she didn't know the Colay. She looked at Lucy more closely and grinned. "Looks like the angels *slapped* you. What happened? You say something cross to them?"

Lucy glared. "It's a *beauty mark*." Snowcap hooted, and Lucy shook her hair forward over her cheek and settled in, stone faced, to listen to what Snowcap had to say.

The girls rested. They would begin their trip to the stables that evening—said Snowcap—but until then, they could relax. They found a sunny spot where the trees were not so dense and sat on their cloaks on the ground. Lucy lit a fire and boiled walnuts for Rob, enough food for a couple of days. Though Lucy didn't want her around and didn't speak to her, Snowcap showed no intention of leaving them alone. As Lucy fed

Rob more of the goat milk, she decided that Snowcap could at least answer a few questions. So Lucy plunged in: "Don't you feel bad helping the Colay? I mean, doesn't that make you a traitor to the Anglish?"

Snowcap looked startled, then jutted out her chin forcefully. "No, of course not. How can a ruler betray her country? I *make* the rules." She deepened her voice. "And I hereby rule that this baby will live if you will help me." She laughed, but then shook her head. "Besides, if the Colay have a savior, I don't believe *he's* it. I don't believe that someone can be a savior who doesn't, well, who doesn't *save*. And he doesn't do anything but lie there and eat and sleep. How can he save you?"

Lucy hadn't really thought of it that way. "When he's older . . ."

"Then I'll worry about him when he's older."

Lucy was a bit stunned. She had meant to ask a question that would make Snowcap feel guilty, but all she had done was allow Snowcap to insult her–and Rob. As if Rob couldn't save the Colay! Lucy wiped the milk off his chin and took a new line of attack. "Snow-Cap," she said, drawing out the syllables. "That's a Colay name."

She hit her target. Snowcap's head jerked back. "It's not at all! It's English!"

Lucy shrugged. "Well, it sounds Colay to me. I thought all the Anglish girls were named Elizabeth. What happened to you?"

Snowcap picked a lone daisy from the small patch of sun-speckled dirt on which the girls were sitting. She twirled it between her fingers. "It's not a *usual* English name," she admitted. "My mum liked fairy stories. There's one in her family about a girl named Snowy

White. She wanted to give me that name, but Da refused. He wanted to name me Capitola, because he thought it was a fit name for a Governor's daughter. And they couldn't agree at all, so they compromised with Snowcap." She looked up at Lucy defiantly. "So it *is* an English name."

Lucy didn't see how that compromise could have pleased either party, but she decided not to pursue it. Two of Snowcap's words had caught her interest. "What's a fairy story?"

"A made-up story, I guess. One with magic in it." Snowcap began to peel the petals off the daisy, one by one. They floated to the ground like tiny moth wings and lay startling white against the dark earth.

"Oh." Lucy was disappointed. She had thought that maybe Snowcap was talking about real stories, true stories, *useful* stories. Of what use were made-up ones? She burped Rob, and he fell asleep against her shoulder.

Snowcap stripped the flower down to its stem and then flicked the stem away. It landed in the nearby shade. "What's your name?" she asked suddenly.

What would it hurt to tell the truth? "Lucy."

"That's an English name!"

"Yes." Lucy realized she knew a story that would make Snowcap stop laughing and acting so smug. She cleared her throat and said, "My parents wanted to name me in honor of peace between the Anglish and the Colay. So when I was born, my village sent a messenger to the Governor and asked for a name. The Governor said Lucy was a good name."

"My *father* named you?"

"If your father was Robert O'Kelly."

Snowcap whistled through her teeth. "Lucy was my grandmother's name. She died in Ireland long before I was born."

"I know."

"Huh. Why didn't they name you Nora, after my mother?"

"The Colay never name babies after living people. It's bad luck."

"Oh." Snowcap sat for a moment without moving. Then she laughed again (*Will she ever be quiet?* thought Lucy) and asked, "So, what's the baby's name? Some dead Englishman? James? Prince Hal? Richard the Lionheart?"

Lucy smiled at Snowcap for the first time, a rather unpleasant smile. "His name's Robert. I call him Rob."

Snowcap did not reply. And she didn't laugh again. She turned and walked off into the woods. Lucy had exactly the silence she'd been hoping for, she and Rob finally alone together. But it didn't feel as good as she'd expected. Lucy thought about her own father and mother and how she missed them both, and she pulled the bark off a twig. Snowcap returned a few moments later with smudged cheeks. They sat in silence and watched the baby sleep.

20

A Man May Be Mistaken

At noon, Philip sent all his pupils outside; they either ate their meals on the stumps in front of the school or they went to their homes to eat. In the past, he had used this hour to take a nap at his desk (he even used an old blanket as a pillow so that his forehead wouldn't have desk marks during the afternoon lessons). Today he made a new resolution: no more noontime naps. He would continue to write. He had to, if he wanted to become a Great Author.

He stretched his fingers and began.

The Tathish Language
By Philip Tudor, linguist and scholar

Tathish, spoken by all the natives of Tathenn and the Colay Islands, is really more like a thieves' cant than an actual language. It is a very simple language, so much so that it is possible for an Englishman nearly to understand a Tathish speaker, though much of the vocabulary and grammar differs from English; and the Tathenlanders have, of course, a much more direct and barbaric style of speaking. They have no written language and therefore no literary arts, no history, no letters.

Tathish seems to me to most closely resemble the language of the Algonquian Indians of New England. Yet it also shares similarities with the language of the ancient Hebrews. But the Colay themselves have never intimated that they know where it is they come from. They do not possess, as I have said, any sense of history.

(Incidentally, Philip had never studied the Algonquian language, but he *had* studied Hebrew briefly, when he was seven years old. As he showed very little aptitude for the ministry and even less for languages, Hebrew was given up after only a few months. He remembered nothing from his lessons.)

The Tathish dialect is, in general, simpler and more limited than English. At the same time, it is complex and quite difficult to master—

His schoolroom door opened. He waved his left hand angrily without even looking up from his writing. "Get out now, you rapscallion, or you'll be writing lines until you are old enough to serve time in Newgate!"

"Ahem."

That was not the response of a student.

Philip looked up quickly. "Oh. Oh my goodness!" He jumped up from his seat and stood nervously behind his desk, elbows tucked close to his body. "So sorry!"

"Quite all right," said Renard. Sir Markham stood, as regally as a reed-thin man could, behind him. "I'm sure you must enjoy your small privacy at noontime." Renard glided toward the desk, carrying a small bundle.

"Writing?" asked Sir Markham.

"Just—just some historical information. For posterity." Philip coughed and stopped talking, thinking how silly it all sounded.

"I'm sure that will be of great interest. To your students," Sir Markham said, drawing near. "However, we are here to discuss something of dire importance." He pointed, and Renard deposited the bundle—which Philip could now see was a sheet of paper and a flattened piece of bark—on the desk with a half bow and a flourish. Sir Markham gazed at the documents and stroked his beard as if posing for a portrait: *The Ruler Ponders Weighty Documents*.

But Philip could see that Sir Markham's hand was shaking, ever so slightly. What was wrong? There was a text here that Philip could not read, a layer of meaning beneath the surface of their conversation. Well, he was sure he'd find out what the problem was when he saw whatever was in that paper. He waited expectantly.

"These"—Sir Markham's voice quavered like his hand—"are a pair of letters we received this morning." He turned to Philip and contorted his face into an agony of concern. "Our darling girl, our Snowcap, has been brutally kidnapped by barbarians."

Renard watched closely, eyes darting from Philip to Sir Markham and back again.

"She—what?" Philip blurted. He wasn't sure what news he'd been expecting, but this was not it. Snowcap kidnapped? By whom? And Snowcap a darling girl? *To* whom? He felt as if he had fallen into a world that was eerily similar to his own but with a few jarring details altered. "Excuse me, sir, but what do you mean?"

Sir Markham's worried expression was so tight it appeared as if his face were going to splinter. "Snowcap disappeared sometime last night; we found these ransom notes late this morning. We—we were hoping you could confirm for us if this note is really from Snowcap."

Sir Markham glanced at Renard, and Renard stepped into the gap in the monologue. "We need to know: Is it her handwriting? And is the other note, as we suspect, from the Colay? Do you also interpret it as a ransom note? Take a look and tell us what you think." He looked at Sir Markham and took a deep breath. "Dear Sir Markham, come. We'll wait outside. You're upset, and Philip needs quiet to look over these documents." To Philip he said, "Please hurry. We need to know that we are reading these papers correctly, so we came, of course, to the most expert reader in Tathenland." Renard laid his hand on Sir Markham's shoulder and guided him firmly out the door.

As soon as the door was shut, Philip groaned and let

his head fall forward on his desk. He wished fervently that he understood people better; he knew he had missed something crucial there.

He looked at the documents.

The note written on the bark used illiterate pictographs such as the Colay drew; Philip could not decipher its meaning completely, but he agreed that the girl pictured looked somewhat like Snowcap and the split crown seemed to indicate a desire for power. Yes, it could be intended to say that Snowcap had been kidnapped and to demand power in exchange for her safe return. It *could* be.

He unrolled the second note, written on birch bark paper, and studied the script closely. It was Snowcap's careless style. And it was certainly her way of dripping ink all over the paper. The note was very short:

Please save me. Or the Colay men say they will hurt me. They threaten me. Please.

Philip was suddenly sorry for Snowcap in a way he had never been before—not merely because she was an orphan and no one liked her, not simply because she was all alone in the world, but because she was scared and in danger. And Philip, in a rare and fleeting moment of truth, understood how she must feel; he had once felt that way himself, locked in a prison cell. He got up and walked to the door, deep in thought.

As he reached to pull open the door, he heard a snippet of conversation through the badly sealed crack. (Sadly, there'd been no master carpenter aboard any of the ships on their voyage.) Sir Markham said, "Things are not going according to plan. What if she manages to find friends to help her?" To which Renard snorted. "Friends? Her?" And then, unctuously, "We've had a tiny, minor setback. There is no flaw with the plan. Don't worry—let me worry for you. You just think ahead to your days of rule." And Sir Markham breathed deeply: "Ah."

Philip felt distinctly uneasy. He knew that eavesdroppers never hear good about themselves, but he hadn't realized that it was equally true that they never hear good of others, either. He'd have to think more about the conversation later—but it certainly sounded like they were not terribly broken up over Snowcap's disappearance. Well, for now, he could still rescue some small writing time. Maybe he could even write about this event. He took two giant steps back, stomped toward the door, and pulled it open.

"Yes," Philip said, as the two men turned to him. "I think you are right. This is definitely Snowcap's handwriting. And while I'm not an expert on Colay pictographs, I certainly agree with your interpretation. The split crown indicates—"

"A coup attempt. Thank you for your help. It will certainly be remembered." Sir Markham pressed his fingers together and shot a glance at Renard.

Renard bowed slightly and raised his eyebrows. "Perhaps you could do us one more favor?"

The noon hour was half flown. Philip sighed and nodded his head.

21

KIDNAPPED!

During the final half of his noon break, Philip wrote out four copies of a notice to be posted at each major Baytown building: the mill, the church (which doubled as an assembly hall), the school, and the courtroom (which doubled as a ballroom each Christmas Eve and Landing Day). His wrist was very tired. He handed the copies to Sir Markham, who rolled them up and handed them to Renard, and they both strode out of the classroom.

Philip could already hear his students gathering outside, waiting for him to call them back to school. He steeled himself; after all, a Great Author kept creating even in the face of tragedy—even when one of his students disappeared in a strange manner. He reread his essay on language, and found that he was confused by his own writing. How could he say that the Colay language was both simple and complex? He tapped his quill pen on the desk, but could think of no way around the problem. Finally, he put a dark red X through the page and set it aside. Maybe it would be easier if he skipped language and moved directly to culture. So he jotted himself a note: *After lessons today: CULTURE.* And he rose and called his students to class.

22

LUCY'S PLAN

The afternoon was waning, and the girls still had no clear plan. Lucy couldn't go into Picle without a plan—it was insane. But Snowcap, who was currently humming and stirring vegetables over a little fire she'd made, did not appear at all concerned. *She's even using my pot to make her stew*, Lucy thought. *She wouldn't get anywhere if she didn't have me. What a worthless Governor she'll be! She can't do anything without help from other people. Not like me.*

Lucy would have to come up with a plan herself. She gathered up Rob, who was whimpering to be fed, and after changing him with Amarrah's rags, she fed him walnut broth, all the while wondering how to rescue a horse that wasn't hers in a town she didn't know filled with people she had to avoid—with a baby strapped to her back.

As she made stew, Snowcap racked her brains. She had never cooked for herself before, but she knew enough to throw the vegetables—a handful of scrawny potatoes, a small bunch of carrots, a parsnip, and an onion (half of what was in her sack)—in boiling water; and she had decided that, no matter how they tasted, she would eat them and not give that awful Colay girl another opportunity to feel superior to her. Besides, she had bigger problems than how to cook vegetables. She needed a better plan to rescue Peat. But the more she thought about how much she needed a plan, the more she could not come up with one. She felt paralyzed. The vegetables fell apart and burned to the bottom of the pot. Snowcap took them off the fire and stirred vigorously, but all that happened was that the burnt bottom crust floated lazily to the top, where it broke into tiny black crumbs and mixed through the mushy vegetables. Snowcap scraped off a piece of bark to make a scoop and began to eat.

Nothing was recognizable; she couldn't tell if she was eating burnt potato or burnt carrot or burnt parsnip. *Is a parsnip still a parsnip if it doesn't look or smell or taste like a parsnip?* she wondered drearily.

Lucy watched Snowcap eat burnt mush and thought, *I wouldn't have even known that she was eating vegetables except that I saw her put them in the pot.* Rob gulped down the walnut broth. She wiped his chin, looked up at Snowcap, and said, "I have an idea."

23

THINKING OF OTHERS

The plan was agreed upon. But Snowcap still had questions. "How will they ever think that you're me? I'm fair and you're dark; I'm thin and you're . . . sturdy." Lucy scowled, but Snowcap continued. "Your face–"

"I'm ugly?"

"I didn't say that."

"You didn't have to. It was in your eyes." Lucy looked away, thinking of the day Rob was born. "I know what people think of me."

"You mean your scar?"

"*Birthmark.*"

"Birthmark, then. It makes you look–interesting."

Snowcap almost apologized for her earlier words but stopped herself just in time. Governors did not apologize—at least, Sir Markham never did. "Tell me more about your plan."

"Fine, Miss Angel's Kiss. There's just one thing first." Lucy hesitated. "If I'm going to have any chance, I can't take Rob with me. You have to take him."

"You want *me* to take the baby? I don't know how to take care of babies! What if he cries?"

"Then you feed him or burp him or change him," Lucy said curtly. "This is harder for me to ask than for you to do. I don't exactly want to give him over to you, even for a short time."

"Then why do it?"

"Because it's safest for him. But you have to promise me . . . if anything goes wrong and I get caught, you'll take him to the desert. That's the very first thing you have to do. Don't wait; don't go back . . . for me or for anything else. Even if we don't manage to get your horse, you have to promise me that you'll take him to the desert. I deserve that promise for what I'm going to do for you."

Snowcap glowered. She did not like promises, and she did not like being told what to do. "Fine. I promise," she muttered.

"Good. But—"

"But what? You want more?"

"How do I know you'll really do it? How can I trust you?"

Snowcap drew herself up to her full height (which was not very tall, but it *was* dramatic). "I don't lie. I know people say lots of things about me, but they don't call me a liar. When I make a promise, I keep it. And I promise to get the baby safely to the desert, no matter what."

Lucy had to rely on Snowcap's word. But Rob! How could she leave him? "You have to tell the desert philosophers that Rob is the last baby to be born on Sunset. And"—she remembered the words of her own promise—"that the Lady on the Gray Mountain sends her greetings to a man named Beno and hopes to see him again soon. Can you remember that?"

"Of course. I'm not stupid." Because she was getting her way, Snowcap grinned. Lucy almost grinned back— but she stopped herself. The Colay did not grin at their captors. At least, *she* didn't.

Snowcap's curiosity kept her talking. "If you get caught, don't you want me to try to rescue you? You could have made me promise to do that, you know. Wouldn't you rather I rescue you than take Rob away to the desert?"

"No," said Lucy, "because you might get caught, and then Rob would get caught. The most important thing is to get him to the philosophers."

"Huh," said Snowcap. "Whenever *I* go anywhere, the most important person is *me*."

"That's because you never think of anyone else," Lucy replied angrily.

Snowcap merely nodded. This talk made her think of her parents, who *had* been able to apologize when they erred—and who had always thought more of her than of themselves. It was the last time, she realized, that someone had cared about her that way. No, there was Adam. He cared about her, too, but it wasn't quite the same as having a mother or father who loved you.

Lucy, meanwhile, remembered her father trying to make a deal with an Anglish stranger—trying and *failing*. She needed some fresh air, away from Snowcap. "I'm taking the baby for a walk. Don't worry; we won't go far."

Snowcap nodded again, still lost in thought.

24

MISSED BY MANY

A notice to be read through the streets of Baytown and to be posted at each public building:

Hear ye, Hear ye: The Precious and Beloved Child Governor, Miss Snowcap Margaret O'Kelly, daughter of the unfortunate late Governor, Robert O'Kelly, and his late wife, Nora, has on this day been atrociously and coldheartedly kidnapped. She must Be Found! The child's Protector and Faithful Servant, Sir Markham, offers a Substantial Reward for her safe return to the palace at Baytown. All Kidnappers will be Severely Punished!

The Baytown crier read the announcement and then posted it for the pleasure of those who could read. People were impressed by the long words (all of which Philip had spelled correctly). It was big news.

But what was even more impressive was that the Protector (and Faithful Servant), Sir Markham, knew that Snowcap had *not* been kidnapped (by *anyone*), because she had addressed a note to Adam saying that she was running away and asking him to take special care of her horse.

Renard had found the note pinned to the door of the stable, and he had read it and burned it and told no one but Sir Markham.

When the notice was posted at the school, which happened shortly after the noon hour, Philip found that he was the only person there who felt any sympathy for Snowcap. Her fellow schoolmates were certainly not weeping at the thought of her capture.

"How exciting! A kidnapping in Baytown." One child actually pounded his desk in glee.

"Now you can't say nothing ever happens here," said another.

"I wonder who did it. Oooh—it's likely someone we know!" Virginia, a fisherman's daughter with a tendency toward melodrama, clapped her hands over her mouth and widened her eyes.

"Or it could be the Colay," said Peter, the baker's son.

"Maybe so," replied the miller's son (sounding hopeful).

"But who would want to kidnap *her*?" asked Peter, who had endured much torture from Snowcap over the years. "And I thought she was sick today. Was she kidnapped from her sickbed?"

"Why did you think she was sick?" asked Philip, who was listening to the talk as he sorted slates.

"Uh—the note. I didn't *mean* to read it. . . ." Peter squirmed a bit.

"Oh my goodness, the note." In all the hubbub of the day, Philip had forgotten. Glad not to be scolded, Peter explained to the others that he had delivered a note from Sir Markham saying that Snowcap was sick.

"But the note wasn't actually from Sir Markham," Philip mused aloud. "It was clearly a forgery."

"It was?" gasped Virginia.

"Then it must have been written by the kidnappers! To make it look like she was sick," concluded Peter.

That explanation didn't seem quite right to Philip. But he didn't want to discuss it with his students. "Right," he said. "Class dismissed."

25

STABLE

On the afternoon of Snowcap's disappearance, Adam stood in the stable, as he often did, currying the government's five horses. These were very special animals, for there were only twenty-four horses in all of Tathenland. As the only official groom on the islands, Adam was responsible for Promoting the Birth of Foals and Caring for Ill Horses. He was, in essence, the unofficial minister of transportation, and Snowcap's calling him a "horse boy" the day before had been most unfair. Under the O'Kellys' rule, he had been a very important and well-respected person, though it is true he was looked down upon in the new regime. Adam didn't mind. He loved his life for what it was, not for what others thought of it.

As he brushed and fed the horses, Adam sang this song:

Oh England, sweet England,
I fear I'll ne'er see you more,
And if I do I'm dreamin' of gallows.
My fingers are rottin', and my bones they are sore.
I wander about right down to death's door.
But if I can just live
To see seven years more,
I will soon bid farewell to Virginny.

It was a good song that gave his voice something to do as his hands brushed the horses' manes and his mind labored over problems. The crew had sung it aboard the *Hopewell* to tease the prisoners, but Adam and Robert O'Kelly had grown to love the song. It made Adam feel strangely both happy and sad, reminding him of how he lost his first home—and how he found his second.

Adam had no rosy illusions about his previous life, yet he did miss it. A poor and illiterate child, he had roamed in the heart of bad London, the youngest member of an extended family of thieves. They spoke their own dialect; had their own special handshakes and hat tippings (those who wore hats); and nested together in small back rooms, hidden from the law. When they needed food or money, they went to work: the children roaming the crowded markets, picking pockets and stealing from stalls; the men creeping out at evening to whisper and plot in pubs or to jump out at lonely dandies on darkened streets; the women visiting men's clubs, doing what looked to Adam like no work at all, but which surely must have been something for they often left drunk men sleeping on curbs and came home with wallets, watches, and fancy handkerchiefs.

Thievery was his family's profession, and they apprenticed him to it with as much seriousness as if he were becoming a horse groom or a bank clerk. As a small boy, Adam was taught to pick pockets and locks, to crawl in and out of tight windows, and to eavesdrop by hunching under tables or in cupboards. It was while he was swaggering casually away from an old man he'd relieved of a purse of coins that a greasy ferret—a pawnbroker, Adam explained to Snowcap, working on the side of the law and a traitor to thieves everywhere—grabbed him by his nape. In a few brief moments, Adam had lost his freedom. Since he was quite young, the Old Bailey judge decided that Adam might mend his ways if sent away from the evil influences of his family. Thus he was clapped into prison and sentenced to be transported to the colonies for seven years.

By this point, Adam's family was broken up: an older brother and sister had already been transported, and his father had been gaoled for highway robbery but died of gaol fever before he could be sentenced to hanging. Adam left behind his mother, two older brothers, two older sisters and their husbands, and various cousins, uncles, aunts, nieces, and nephews. He had begged the judge to let him stay and had pointed out that he was only eight, too young to transport.

The attorney had snorted. "Nonsense. This so-called child is at least twelve, as you can tell by looking at the shape of his head and the darkness of his hair. He's just small."

On the basis of this scientific evidence, he was falsely registered as a twelve-year-old convict and transported.

When he first told Snowcap this story, she was ten years old. "How bad did you want to stay in London?" she had asked. "Would you have—eaten worms?" It was the worst she could think of.

"Sure. I wish I could've done as two of my older brothers did. They raised their paws for medical experiments, and they got to stay in London. Cyrus let the doctors saw his leg off."

Snowcap was amazed. "Why did they saw it off?"

"They were testing pain medicines and poultices. Wanted to see if they worked. They didn't." Adam rubbed Peat's neck as he fed him from a bucket of oats. "Not as Cyrus said."

"What did he do when he got freed?"

"Learnt to hoof it with a crutch. And went into a new branch of the business. Too hard to shimmy through windows."

"And your other brother? How did he get freed?"

"Edgar? He let 'em take his eardrum. Dunno." He anticipated Snowcap's question. "It's some tidbit inside your ear that makes you hear."

"Is he deaf then?"

"Nah. Just hard of hearin'. He still got one good ear, see. He does the Selling of Acquired Goods, along with my mum." Adam shook his head and moved down to feed Acorn (Peat's mother), the horse in the next stall. "I don't know what them doctors ever wanted with that eardrum. But it saved Edgar from transport, so he gave it."

"Transport isn't so bad," said Snowcap.

"You say that," said Adam, "since you've never been.

What if you had to leave your only home and kin, all with no promise you'd ever return? You'd feel shabby, you would."

"That's what you think," said Snowcap. "*I'd* think it was an adventure." Then she had stalked away, deliberately tipping over the oats bucket as she passed. Even then, she did not like to be contradicted.

Snowcap had always been strong-willed and demanding, traits her parents had leavened with regular bedtimes, unconditional love, and lots of outdoor activity; but after her parents' deaths, she was almost uncontrollable with grief. She realized early on that her Protector and his steward were not interested in her welfare. Feeling alone and unloved, she became angry and, soon enough, cruel.

Adam, however, tried to treat her as if she were his little sister. He knew she felt lonely, and he felt sorry for her (though he also knew if he told her that, it would make her furious). He had loved her parents. He loved Snowcap, too—not only for their sakes, but also for who she was: her strong will, her determination, her way with horses. He loved her even though as time went on, she became less and less easy to love.

For Adam, the way to show love was to talk. He talked to Snowcap whenever he could and told her whatever stories she would listen to. He taught her songs—including the mournful convicts' song—and generally gave her a much different picture of London life than Philip taught in school. Adam's London was foggy and grimy, and his streets were full of urchins and thieves. His Londoners frequented dirty pubs, attended hangings and frenzied market days, and donated loved ones to Newgate Prison with unfortunate regularity. They dodged the law, moved frequently from hovel to hovel, and feared entering the poorhouse (or worse) one day soon.

Surprisingly, Snowcap loved to hear Adam's stories about London, especially stories of his own family. "Historical tales," he called them. His maternal grandmother had been quite famous: Mary Young (alias Jenny Diver), Receiver of Acquired Goods, known throughout London as one of the best in the business. She was transported to America several times, but her gang always managed to smuggle her back to London. All Adam's information about America had come from this wonderful grandmother, who did not see the New World as a desirable place to pursue her profession.

"Why?" asked Snowcap. "Does no one steal in America?"

"It's not that. It's just—there weren't much there *to* steal. So it weren't a lack of desire as much as a lack of material. But that was awhile back now. P'rhaps it's changed."

Snowcap was intrigued by the size of the families Adam described: large, sprawling, disjointed—and as varied as summer storms. Some were cruel, mean, petty, vicious; others, like Adam's own family, were loving and close-knit, working and living together, taking pride in whatever the family did. When Snowcap once asked him what he missed most about London, Adam replied without hesitation: "My mum. And my brothers and sisters left there. All my kin."

"But—they're all thieves."

"Ah," said Adam, grinning. "And so am I, too, kid. We're all thieves here. That's something worth rememberin', no matter what you learnt in school."

Snowcap had stuffed this conversation in the back of her memory, from which it crawled out at odd times to pester her. The night she ran away, Adam's words slunk back into her thoughts as she stole over the garden wall; they materialized again later as she crept through the woods, trying to dream up a plan for nabbing Peat. *We're all thieves here. That's something worth remembering.*

Adam wasn't thinking of that particular conversation as he curried Highwayman, the oldest of the horses, on the afternoon of Snowcap's disappearance. But he *was* thinking of Snowcap and their argument of the previous day, wondering what to do about her rudeness. Someone needed to teach her ways of being respectful. He worried that she had no real friends at all—only people who groveled—and he didn't trust Sir Markham and that sneaky steward—*Oh! Think about the devil, and there he is.* Renard hovered at his elbow.

"A bit jumpy, aren't you? What's the problem?" said Renard.

"No problem," Adam replied. "Just—don't sneak up. It scrambles the horses."

"Hmm." Renard took a notebook out of his breast pocket and wrote in it, muttering loud enough for Adam to hear: "Jumpy. Defensive. Hiding something?"

Renard was obviously up to some kind of game, and Adam decided he wouldn't stoop to ask what it was. He went back to brushing Highwayman's thick coat.

Renard stood watching for a long, long time. At last he said impatiently, "Don't you wonder why I'm here?

Or"—he scribbled in his notebook again—"perhaps you already know why I'm here?"

"No, I don't. But I'm sure you'll tell me if it's somethin' I need to know."

"Yes, I will." Renard jotted a last thought, then he pulled a sheet of paper out of his breast pocket and handed it to Adam.

Adam didn't even glance at it. "I'm not a jarkman." He kept brushing.

"What? Oh, that's right—you can't read. Allow me." With highly exaggerated slowness, he read the note from Snowcap saying she'd been kidnapped. "Philip agrees it's her handwriting. The poor dear." Adam raised his eyebrows at the use of the word "dear," but Renard, pulling another note out of his breast pocket, didn't notice. "Here's the other. From the kidnappers themselves. Even *you* can read this one. It's written by a wholly illiterate people." He showed Adam the bark with the two pictures.

Adam put his brush down and looked at this note. After studying it, he said (with exaggerated slowness), "So—you—think—the—Colay—are—behind—this?"

"Undoubtedly." Renard sneered, tapping his neck with his small, strong fingers. "But they probably have an accomplice within the palace, hmm?" To Adam's constant disgust, Sir Markham and Renard insisted upon calling the O'Kelly home "the palace," although it was nothing at all like what Adam had heard about Windsor Castle, outside of London. It was really just a large house.

"An accomplice?" Adam repeated. What game was this, exactly?

"If you have any suspicions, you must let us know. Meanwhile, don't go anywhere. We want everyone to stay close to the palace and keep their eyes and ears open."

"But shouldn't we be lookin' for Snowcap?"

Renard appeared faintly surprised—and just a small bit worried. "No, horse boy, we already *are* looking for her. And we will find her. Now, please excuse me. I must question the *other* servants."

After Renard left, Adam remained at the stable, singing old songs from England as he brushed down the horses and thought over Renard's news. Something was not right. Snowcap, unlikable as she might be, was not an easy person to fool or to force to do anything against her will. How had she been kidnapped? Adam didn't trust either Sir Markham or Renard—they knew something about the O'Kellys' deaths that they weren't telling, of that he was sure, and now, on top of this, Snowcap's mysterious disappearance was too much to believe.

Adam moved on to Peat, who shook his head and whinnied in appreciation. *Ah*, Adam thought, *p'rhaps—just p'rhaps—Snowcap wasn't kidnapped at all. P'rhaps she simply scoured off.* And if so, she would certainly come back for Peat. Adam would watch for her and try to help her, as he always did. He sang on.

26

THE STORY OF A GOOD HORSE

The first thing Philip did after dismissing his students was to look at the note he'd received that morning—

> Snowcap is sik and wil not be at lessons today.
> Plese exquse her.
> Signed Sir MarkHam

Clearly the note was written by Snowcap, so—how to explain it? He thought and thought until he came up with an explanation that satisfied him and kept him from having to think anymore: Snowcap must have been planning to play sick, and then she'd been kidnapped instead. Yes, it was a big coincidence, but what other explanation was as simple?

Excellent! He'd solved that problem, and now he could get to work. He felt for Snowcap, he did—but there was nothing he could do for her. He needed to be brave, to continue his own quest. He would write, every day, until he wrote Something Important. Next: Culture.

An hour later, Philip was sitting morosely in the empty schoolroom with a blank piece of paper. Well, to be honest, the paper was not *quite* blank. At the top perched the word CULTURE in large capital letters, dripping with ornate decorations of shrubs, flowers, and oversized butterflies. Near the bottom of the page floated the word FISH, draped with a knobby net. Around this net swam a school of small, lumpy creatures with fins as big as wings—creatures that did not remotely resemble the fish that swam the waters surrounding Tathenland. Straining upward through the fishnet, apparently growing out of the sea bottom, a stringy vine crept along the entire left margin of the page—or, what would've been the left margin, had there been any text to its right. This sulky vine blossomed with drooping globular flowers: mutant hydrangea? Near the top end of the vine, the flowers slowly transformed into the petaled faces of his pupils, too-round and poorly drawn, but recognizable as they peered out from the leaves. Snowcap's face was the crowning bud on the vine, glaring at him from the top of the page.

Writing, Philip decided, was strenuous.

He took out a new piece of paper—hand pressed from

wood pulp, uneven and stiff—and stared at it. Fresh paper, even this crude stuff, was one of the most beautiful (if terrifying) things in the world, full of promise. He turned the paper over and over in his hands, brushing his palms against it and feeling its slight weight on his fingertips. It reminded him of spring buds about to open, sunshine not quite yet spilling into a doorway, a bird about to take flight. Yes, a water bird: maybe a loon. A loon about to land, on a clear pond. Or maybe paper was the clear pond itself, glassy and empty on the surface but with life teeming in its belly. Yes, a new piece of paper was like a clear pond, a clear pond with a loon about to land on it. He smiled and imagined the loon trailing a wake across the water's placid surface. He imagined skipping a stone across the loon's wake—something he'd never successfully done, but one could always imagine? The stone would hiss lightly each time it kissed the water, and the ripples would radiate out in all directions as the stone sped away from him into infinity.

Then Philip shook himself. He was wasting time again. This would not do. He tried very hard to concentrate, but his mind kept drifting away from the subjects at hand (*CULTURE* and *FISH*?) and turning toward Snowcap. Where was she? Was she safe and . . . alive?

There was nothing he could do to help find her, he was quite sure. But now, sitting in the lonely, slowly dimming classroom, he couldn't think of anything else but Snowcap—Snowcap in trouble and afraid.

Right, he thought, *I'll compose something about Snowcap.*

He sat, staring out the classroom doorway into the

late-afternoon street. What could he say about her? He searched his mind and found one good thing about Snowcap: she loved her horse.

Snowcap Margaret O'Kelly's horse, Peat, was a beautiful coal-black mount who ran swifter than the wind. He was said to be a kind horse and a clever one, friendly to all in the stable.

No, he thought, scratching through the lines. *I need to write about Snowcap, not her horse.* He began again:

Snowcap Margaret O'Kelly, the Child Governor, was born on Tathenn in the year of our Lord 1775. She was kind—

Philip chewed his pen and absently wiped ink on his chin. He didn't want to insult the memory of Governor and Nora O'Kelly, but he also did not want to lie.

—to animals. Her particular friend was Peat, her horse. She took him out each fine day and spoke softly to him at all times. She gave Adam, the groom, fresh apples for Peat, and Peat ate them gently out of Adam's hand—

Philip broke off. He was writing about Peat again. Surely he could think of something else nice to say about Snowcap.

But he could think of nothing. She was not good, nor kind (to anyone human), nor thoughtful. She was not even a good speller. No, she was a terrible speller.

Oh! Philip threw down his pen, jumped up, and almost knocked over his ink bottle. The note that Sir

Markham and Renard showed him from Snowcap—she hadn't written that note! She couldn't have! He closed his eyes and pictured the words:

> Please save me. Or the Colay men say they will hurt me. They threaten me. Please.

All the words were spelled correctly.

Philip paced. If Snowcap hadn't written the note, then who had? And why?

As the last long light of afternoon flitted across Philip's desk, he glanced once more at his writing and noticed that he had abruptly ended his essay with *Adam's hand*.

Adam! If anyone knew what to do—and would care enough about Snowcap to do it—that would be Adam.

27

THE FOOL AND THE HORSE BOY

Adam had eaten dinner with the housemaid, the cook, and the gardener, all of whom could talk of nothing but Snowcap's disappearance. The cook, an especially good-hearted and forgiving woman (who'd managed a house of thieves in London), felt sorry for Snowcap in spite of everything she'd done to ruin meal after meal that the poor woman prepared. The gardener and the maid (a former buyer of stolen fish and a stealer of clothing, respectively) were more sparing with their sympathy: they felt sorry for Snowcap, but they felt even *more* sorry for her kidnappers, who now had to put up with her. Adam was silent, slowly chewing and considering.

After dinner he went up to his quarters above the stable, picked up his bedding, and headed back down. He had decided to sleep near Peat, in case Snowcap returned. As he came down the ladder, he saw Philip the Tutor peering in the open stable door and calling his name softly.

"'Lo," Adam answered.

Philip turned and fluttered his hands. "My dear boy, you startled me!"

"Sorry. Everyone's so jumpy today. Wha'd you want, sir?"

Philip dropped his arms. "I need help. I've a problem—a question—a *concern*, really, about Snowcap. And I think that you may be the only one who can help."

After twelve years on the island and many births (and, of course, some deaths), there were 285 English residents of Tathenland; as this is a rather small number for a country, everyone knew one another fairly well. Yet, while Philip knew that Adam was levelheaded and trustworthy (and Snowcap's staunchest friend), Adam and Philip had never really spoken before. Adam hadn't learned to write beyond his name (in large capitals), and he could read only a few signs (*bakery, pub, jeweler's, gaol*)—useful knowledge in London, but not on Tathenn, which was so small that no one deemed signs necessary. Adam didn't normally like to converse with educated persons such as Philip; they often spoke of things that didn't seem important.

But in Tathenland, Adam and Philip were equals: both held important positions in the government. Some would have argued that Adam's position was more important, for the horses on the island were a precious commodity, more so than the children, if truth be told; the horses were essential to planting and harvesting. Much of Adam's importance, however, was lost on Philip because he was scared of horses. (Philip wouldn't have confessed this, but one of the primary reasons he hadn't wanted to inherit his father's old horse was because he was too terrified to ride the poor, dilapidated creature.) So, Adam had stayed away from Philip's school, and Philip had stayed away from Adam's stable. Now they were standing together, and Philip was asking Adam for help.

Philip flapped his hands again and glanced around furtively. "Where can we talk?"

"In here." Adam motioned to the open stable door.

Philip eyed it pensively. "Are the—the animals—loose in there?"

Adam looked puzzled. "No. They're in stalls. But you can peep at them."

"Oh, no, no. That won't be necessary." Philip took a deep breath. "Let's go inside and talk."

Adam led the way to an empty stall—next to Peat's, though Philip didn't know that—and spread out his blanket. "Hoist yourself down."

Philip sat awkwardly on the blanket. Adam lay across from him on his stomach, resting on his elbows, twisting a piece of straw between his fingers. His pigtail fell forward in a sweep of thick brown that Philip envied. When Philip was settled and his bones had stopped creaking, Adam said, "You have news about Snowcap?"

Philip cleared his throat. "She hasn't been kidnapped by the Colay."

Adam nodded.

"You knew this already?" A horse neighed, and Philip shivered.

"No. I suspicioned. That's just Bridewell; don't worry. She always chats when someone new comes in the stable."

"Ah." Philip shifted but did not relax. He explained about the forged kidnapping note.

Adam nodded again. "Then I think we know what's happened, eh?"

Philip was bewildered. "I think we know only what *hasn't* happened."

Adam dropped the straw he'd been twirling. "Well, if Snowcap didn't scribble that note, then someone else did. The Colay don't write. And the only two forgers on the island are you and Renard. If you didn't do it, then it seems to me that Renard *did*. Besides," he added reflectively as Philip sat in stunned silence, "they say you only know how to do signatures. For an entire document, you'd have to get Renard." He looked up at Philip. "So there you have it."

Philip asked shakily, "Is that really what people say?"

"No offense intended. They say you're a rum speller."

"Ah. Thank you," said Philip, feeling unusually small.

"It seems to me that if Renard's involved, then so is Sir Markham. Those two go together like mosquitos and swamps. And it only follows that they might have snabbled Snowcap themselves. In which case, we need to scout around here for her, maybe in the cellar or the oubliette. Or—it's possible they don't know where she is, either. She might've scoured off."

"Well, that could explain why they weren't too upset . . . and the note about being sick."

"What's that?" Adam asked sharply.

"Oh—it might be that she pretended to be sick because she planned to run away. Do go on." Philip decided not to mention his own carelessness and eavesdropping.

"If she's scampered, she's sure to come here. For her horse." Adam stood up decisively and brushed his pigtail back over his shoulder. "That's settled, then. You want to wait here or go inside?"

"Go inside the mansion? Why?"

"To check the cellar and the oubliette, like I said. And one of us ought to wait here. In case she turns up."

"Uh, y-yes." Things were moving rather rapidly for Philip. Which was the lesser of the two evils? To stay in the stable, surrounded by vicious horses, or go into the house and run the risk of meeting up with Sir Markham or Renard? His greater fear won out. "I'll go inside," he muttered.

Adam nodded. "I'll wait here. Come right back. Do you know where the oubliette is?"

"I'll find it." Philip squared his narrow shoulders as best he could, tucked in his elbows, and marched off.

28

A Spy Behind the Curtain

As Philip neared the house, he slowed his pace. Why had he agreed to go? Was he really risking his life, his future, for Snowcap? But she was in trouble, and she needed help. Maybe she'd be so grateful that forever after she would behave in school and treat him with the utmost respect. She might even reward him—she could found a printer's shop in his name? It was about time that the citizens of Tathenland began publishing books. Maybe they could hire little Colay children to carve the etchings, and Philip could melt down some old pots to make type letters. Just a small press, nothing fancy, of course.

Daydreaming, he wandered through the kitchen garden and entered the quiet house through the kitchen door. He had been inside the Governor's Mansion (as he liked to call it) only once before, at a pleasant get-to-know-you dinner with the O'Kellys when he had been appointed Head (and only) Tutor; Snowcap had been full of energy but polite nonetheless, radiant in her parents' attention, and the dinner had included bread pudding (his favorite dish) and good conversation and had ended with a long, chatty tour of the house, with eight-year-old Snowcap swinging between her parents' arms in the Great Hall. Philip relied on that tour now. He could hear cleaning-up-and-getting-ready-for-bed noises in distant rooms, but no one was in the kitchen, though a low fire burned in the grate. He pressed his ear to the passageway door. Hearing nothing, he cracked open the door and stepped cautiously into the dark hall. The oubliette was the most logical hiding place. Quaking with fear, he shuffled along the wall in the shadows. As he shuffled, he racked his brains, trying to remember exactly where the oubliette was located (not his favorite part of the tour). Where was its little trapdoor? It was somewhere near the end of the hallway. Or was it in the entryway closet?

Feeling his way down the dim hallway, Philip ran his fingers over a tapestry that took up much of the south wall. He stopped and squinted at it in awe, for he remembered seeing it when it had first been completed, two years earlier, as part of a celebration of ten years on Tathenn. It was the single part of the festivities that impressed Philip as grand, artistic, worthy of England. The tapestry pictured three English ships sailing triumphantly into the Baytown harbor while tiny Colay people gathered on shore, waving. From the mouth of one of the Colay men floated a bubble that said "Come here and help us!" Beautiful, brightly colored birds—which did not exist anywhere in Tathenland (or, probably, the world)—soared overhead. Philip admired the artwork immensely, and he stood for a moment, lost in his appreciation of the finer things.

Suddenly the door to the dining room—only a few yards in front of him—swung open. Philip jumped back, felt for the tapestry, and squeezed himself behind it. It covered him like a thick curtain, leaving only the tops of his shoes showing, and if he were lucky, no one would see them in the shadows. He willed himself to be invisible and not to shake.

Footsteps sounded in the hallway. Someone was coming toward him. Then he heard voices, muffled through the thick cloth but still recognizable: Sir Markham and Renard! "We must find the brat tonight," said Sir Markham. "Of course, your Highness," replied Renard. The footsteps disappeared down the hallway.

Philip sank to the floor in relief, causing the tapestry to bulge conspicuously at the bottom. The Protector and steward were looking for a brat, and that could mean only Snowcap. But that also meant they didn't know where Snowcap was! They weren't hiding her in the house. Philip's first feeling was relief for himself: he could leave the house without having to find the oubliette or search the dank cellar. He crawled down the hallway and back through the kitchen and into the garden, moving much faster than when he entered.

In the garden, he realized that their problems were

by no means solved. He and Adam still had no idea where Snowcap was. They would have to wait in the stables for her to return. The prospect of sitting among the horses was so terrifying that he considered going home. *No.* As levelheaded as Adam was, he couldn't rescue Snowcap all by himself (especially if any reading were involved), and no one else seemed about to help. *Besides*, Philip told himself, *one can't always live in fear. Especially a Great Author.* He tossed his head—the first time in his life he'd ever done so—and headed for the stables. He would wait there with Adam.

29

THE CRIME OF
HORSE RESCUING

While Philip was looking for Snowcap, the girls embarked on their plan for horse stealing. They exchanged
cloaks and slid over the West Wall carefully and quietly,
Snowcap carrying Rob (who was, thank Providence,
sleeping) bound tightly to her stomach. Even with the
added burden of the baby, Snowcap moved nimbly;
Lucy followed almost as silently, if not as gracefully. The
night was bright and clear, but no one saw them as they
retraced Snowcap's steps back to the big house.

In the large flower garden behind the house,

Snowcap waited—hidden in a clump of lilacs—while Lucy, following Snowcap's directions, walked toward the kitchen garden. She worried that Rob would wake and cry, but she pushed that fear to the back of her mind and focused on the task at hand: to get two Anglish men to chase her. Snowcap had described one as tall and bearded and the other as smaller and snide, but Lucy decided that as soon as anyone of any description began chasing her, she'd run. She wouldn't wait around to identify them.

She had just opened the gate when she heard a rustling and saw, in fact, a tall bearded man and a smaller hunched man illuminated for a brief second in the moonlight as they rose up from behind a bush. Something looked familiar . . . but she didn't have time to think about it. The smaller man pointed at her, and the taller one whispered loudly and bitterly, "It's her! Snowcap!"

Lucy turned and sprinted, everything cleared from her mind except her role in the plan. Dodging and weaving, she kept in and out of sight for several minutes as she led her pursuers south through town. When she got out of town (following Snowcap's instructions exactly), she passed a large oak tree and then ducked into the first big ditch on the right, where she found the hollowed log that Snowcap had assured her would be there (Snowcap had discovered it two weeks earlier when out riding Peat). Snowcap, slight as she was, would have slid easily into the log, but for Lucy it was a tight squeeze, and in the end, her head simply would not fit. So she burrowed her head into the mulchy leaves lying in the stagnant ditch water. Two sets of feet came near her, and two heavy sticks thwacked the bushes along the ditch. She held her breath and tried to become like the mud. *Thunk.*

Snowcap waited until she heard the slam of the kitchen garden gate and Lucy's pounding run. She waited for the footsteps chasing Lucy to fade away. She waited a few minutes more, and then she sneaked behind the barn, where she climbed a young tree and crawled through the back window into the grain shed, as she had done many times before (though never with a baby bound to her front). From there she crept into the main stable, to Peat's stall. She nestled his neck and shushed him, and— good horse that he was—he did not make a sound. She slid the door open and tiptoed out of the stable, so quietly that no one heard them until the last second, when an urgent voice whispered, "Ho!" Without waiting to see who it was, Snowcap leapt on Peat's back and bolted away.

Even as they ran, she kept Peat as quiet as she could, racing on the grass rather than on the streets. Yet running horses make noise even in the best of circumstances, and Snowcap knew that her pursuers, though not as fast as Peat, would have little trouble trailing them toward the West Wall. *Never mind,* thought Snowcap. *Once we're over the wall and into the woods, we'll lose them easily.* Then she gasped. How would they get over the wall? Peat couldn't climb it!

Snowcap leaned left to turn Peat south, thinking that they could run along the wall until they found an opening somewhere, a section in disrepair; or if need be, they could follow the wall until it ended, far south in the plantations, and then go around it and head northwest, back into the woods. But Peat would not be turned. He sped toward the wall, gathered his huge body together, and—at the last moment, when Snowcap thought surely they would crash—he leapt, higher than she thought possible, and cleared the wall with a handbreadth to spare.

The most amazing thing was that Rob, tied to Snowcap's chest, slept through the entire adventure.

Snowcap arrived back at the boat elated: the plan had worked! While she waited for Lucy, she let Peat graze on the banks and untied Rob from her chest. And *waited*. After a while, Rob began to squirm and cry, so she fed him leftover walnut mush. Then she changed him and bathed him, as she'd seen Lucy do. Then washed the changing cloths and draped them over the back of the boat to dry. Then sang fourteen songs, three of them twice. Changed and fed him again. Walked up and down the bank to lull the baby back to sleep. Finally, when it was almost morning, she curled around Rob in the bottom of the boat. But she couldn't sleep. Where was Lucy? Rob whimpered, and she stroked his forehead. She remembered her promise. She'd never had to care for anyone else before. How would she do it now?

Just before dawn, Snowcap heard the crunching sound of footsteps, and when she peeked over the side of the boat, there was Lucy! Bedraggled and slathered in dried mud, with a giant welt on the crown of her head. She swayed on the bank.

Snowcap sat up. "What happened to you? What took so long?"

"No one got me."

"Right. I can see that. But what happened?" Lucy

swayed again, and Snowcap reached out her hand. Lucy took it, climbed into the boat, and eased herself down. She looked questioningly at Rob, curled on the bottom of the boat, and Snowcap said, "Sound asleep. But you're a mess. Who got your head?"

"The log wasn't big enough—my head stuck out. There were two Anglish men. One snapping, one hissing."

"That'd be them, all right."

"They had big sticks, and they thwacked around trying to find me. Their sticks found my head. But I didn't move, not an eyelash, so they didn't know it was my head. And pretty soon they went away."

"What took you so long to get here, then?"

"They thunked me pretty hard. I fell asleep for a while. I'm still kind of woozy." Lucy touched her head gingerly and winced. Snowcap winced with her.

"You've got a little blood—"

"That's all right." Lucy wiped her face off with Snowcap's dirty cloak, looked down at it, shrugged, took it off, and handed it back to Snowcap. Then she curled next to Rob as if to doze off.

"Oh, no, you don't!" Snowcap shook her and Lucy looked up, sleep already in her eyes. "We have to move, right now. In case they're following."

"Just a couple of hours."

"Fine—if you want to get caught."

Lucy grimaced and heaved herself slowly up and out of the canoe. She said several words in Colay that Snowcap didn't know but guessed weren't polite. Holding Rob, Lucy swayed on the creek bank while Snowcap repacked their knapsacks and hid the canoe by sinking it with stones—they couldn't take Peat in a canoe.

Then Snowcap tied both knapsacks on her back, took the baby out of Lucy's unresisting arms and tied him to her chest, and led Lucy and Peat out of camp.

It was quickly clear, however, that Lucy needed rest. After she stumbled the third time, Snowcap said tentatively, "You can't ride my horse; he'll only let me. But if you put your hand in Peat's mane . . ."

Lucy stared at her, a small trickle of blood still easing down the side of her face, staining the handprint on her cheek.

"It seems strange, but if I'm tired or hurt, I hold on to his mane and walk along next to him, and he gives me . . . He helps me," she finished lamely.

Lucy continued to stare; her head was pounding like the surf in a storm, and she felt she could barely hear. "*Horse magic?*"

"Just try it!" Snowcap grabbed Lucy's right hand, and Lucy jerked away so hard she almost fell backward. But then—not really sure why—she walked over to the horse and rested her hand on his shoulder.

"Dig the hand in. I know it sounds crazy," Snowcap said, "but it works. For me, anyway."

They walked a little more, a girl on each side of Peat. Snowcap, her hand twined in Peat's mane, could feel warmth and peace almost as a physical sensation running up her arm. But Lucy, her hand also twisted in the mane, could feel only the ache that she'd felt since the night in the statue garden. She stumbled again, then removed her hand from Peat. *As if a horse could help!* Out of habit, her fingers traveled to her luck pouch, and she remembered the lifestone hidden there. She pulled it out and held it in her right hand; immediately she felt more clearheaded. The pain from the thunking was still there (as was the pain in her hand), but she knew she could go on.

Rob slept cozily on Snowcap's chest. The girls walked in silence, Lucy holding the stone and beginning to sweep her mind of the pounding surf, and Snowcap gingerly (and then more boldly) exploring a new idea. For as she walked, one hand entangled in Peat's mane and the other resting gently on Rob's head, Snowcap realized she felt—*good*. It was a strange feeling to be needed, to take care of other people. The nicest feeling she'd had in a very long while. And she had Peat; somehow everything was better with a horse around.

When Rob awoke, midmorning, with a wet bottom and an empty belly, Snowcap decided they could rest for a few minutes. Lucy sat down and changed Rob while Snowcap got the food ready—without burning very much of it. After eating, Lucy felt well enough to declare that she'd carry the baby.

But even becoming less needed didn't put a damper on Snowcap's mood. She still had Peat, and she felt magnanimous and talkative. As they started walking again, she thanked Lucy for helping her rescue the horse.

"You mean steal."

"I mean rescue. *My* horse."

"Don't thank me. I didn't do it because I wanted to." Lucy shifted Rob in his sling and trudged along at a safe distance from Peat.

"Well, it was still a brave thing to lead those villains off on a chase. And to have them thunk you."

"Bastia says I'm tough as goats' teeth."

"Who's Bastia?"

"Our village midwife."

"Goats have very ugly teeth."

Lucy frowned. "That's not what she meant."

With rare tact, Snowcap changed the subject. "Are the stories about the wild animals in the forest true?"

"That depends which stories you've heard."

"Why don't you just tell me whatever stories you know?" Snowcap was getting exasperated with Lucy's unwillingness to talk, but she stayed in a good mood from the successful rescue. She even slowed her pace to walk beside Lucy rather than in front of her.

"There's not much to tell: There are animals in the woods. Wild pups. They're very small—just bigger than rats—and vicious, and they attack in packs."

"Like wolves, only smaller?"

"I suppose," said Lucy, who did not know what a wolf was. (Neither did Snowcap, but she had once heard a story about a whole herd of wolves that attacked a girl her age and ate her up, merely because she was wearing a red cloak and had wandered off the trail. Or something like that. Foolish girl.)

"Anyway," Lucy continued, feeling better as she talked, "if we see them, we should climb a tree or swim away." She paused to move a branch out of her path, then added, "I'm surprised we haven't seen them already."

"I wonder where the wild pups come from," Snowcap said. "Why do they live only on Tathenn?"

"They've always been here," said Lucy. She repeated part of the story Amarrah had told her. "They used to be dogs. They lived with us; they were our friends—"

"They lived with the Colay? And what do you mean that they 'used to be dogs'? Either they're dogs or they're not!"

"Don't interrupt. They lived on the island of Tathenn with the Colay, my ancestors, and helped take care of our goats. But then the people had a bad year, several bad years." Her voice deepened, just the way Amarrah's had when she told the story. "Famine. And everyone was hungry, and there was no food for the dogs. So some of the dogs ran into the woods and grew wild. This was a long time ago. The dogs have lived in the woods ever since; they don't want to come back to us. Over many generations, they've grown smaller and more vicious, and they've eaten almost every animal living in the woods, except the ones that can fly or climb trees. When we used to live on Tathenn, they would sneak into villages and eat our goats, and once in a while . . ."—she paused and lowered her eyes just as Amarrah had—"they would even eat people. But they used to belong with us. And then they changed."

"They've changed? That's impossible. If they are pups now, then they've always been pups. Never dogs! Besides, we didn't learn that story in school. That's not in any of my histories."

"Well, I learned it," said Lucy stubbornly. "We have different histories."

"Tell me more about the famine."

"No. It's not a good story to tell right now."

Snowcap snorted and walked ahead of Lucy again as they traveled west and south.

30

TRAVELING COMPANY

In the stable, Adam and Philip had waited silently in the stall next to Peat for Snowcap. The horses nickered and eventually quieted. Philip slept heavily despite the horses. Adam drifted in and out of light sleep.

When Adam heard—almost too late—a slight rustle, he whispered, "Ho!" but girl and horse raced away. Adam roused Philip, and they followed the sound of Peat's hooves to the West Wall, arriving just in time to see, in the distance, Peat and Snowcap make their beautiful and terrifying leap.

The two men drew up short at the wall.

"Wait here," said Adam and ran back toward the last

house they had passed. He returned with a bundle tied up in a blanket. "Some food I snaffled from a larder. Also a blanket and rope."

"Stolen?" Philip was aghast.

"Here we go," said Adam, ignoring him. He tossed the bundle over the wall and then began to climb.

"Wait! Surely you're not—I mean—"

"We've got to find Snowcap before anyone else does." Adam straddled the ledge and reached down his hand to help Philip over. "And before the pups do."

"Pups?" Philip jerked his hand away. "They're real?"

"Of course. Wha'd you think?"

"I thought—just stories?" Philip hesitantly raised both his hands, and Adam grasped them.

"Up and over." Pulling and pulling, Adam dragged Philip's awkward form over the wall. On the other side they rested, gasping, and then began to walk—navigating by moonlight. Adam carried the pack on his back, tracking Snowcap and Peat's trail of broken twigs and crushed leaves. Philip's contribution was to slow the men to a snail's pace with his bad night vision, poor reflexes, and fear of the dark.

As they hiked along, occasionally slapping away mosquitos, Adam asked, "Have you ever reckoned how you'd have rubbed on if we'd wrecked in America instead of Tathenland?"

Philip, who *had* wondered (many times) answered, "No."

Far in the distance, pups howled.

After a brief pause, Adam continued, "I don't know what I'd've done, if we'd actually landed in America. I don't think I could've stood for it, being someone's barnacled valet." He shook his head. "I don't have the—what's the word?—the *temper'ment* to be a prisoner. P'rhaps I'd have scrapped up a mutiny. . . ."

"Mutinies take place at sea. You mean a revolution, young man." Philip's voice turned back into a schoolteacher's.

Adam laughed good-naturedly. "So, a revolution, then."

"A revolution would never work in America. I've read about the colonists; they don't have the *temperament* for it. You'd never get away with it." Philip swatted another mosquito. "Be glad you ended up here."

"Are *you*?"

Though he'd thought plenty about the *what if's* of landing in America, Philip hadn't thought about this question before. "I guess I am glad. Overall, things here are good. Well, they *were*, when the Governor . . ." He trailed off and waved his hands helplessly around him. Everything was wrong now; what else could explain why he was trudging through a wild pup-infested forest to find a bratty girl he didn't even like?

Adam nodded. "Right." They kept following Snowcap's trail.

Morning fled. Noon paused, took a breath, and sprinted away. The men stopped briefly to eat bread and drink from a stream and then pressed on, Adam once again leading the way. He was enjoying the rare opportunity to speak to a person rather than to a horse, even a person who suffered the disadvantage of being educated.

"What d'you want most of all? For yourself, I mean?" asked Adam.

What did Philip want except to be a writer? That was

it, he supposed; he might as well admit it, as silly as it sounded out here in the woods. "I hope to someday be included in the Parthenon of Great Authors." He paused. Something sounded wrong. "Or do I mean Pantheon? Panopticon?"

Adam shrugged. "It's all Greek to me." Still, he considered the statement. "Are you sayin' what you want is to be famous?"

Philip thought carefully. "I—yes. A famous writer, that is."

Adam raised his hand and pushed brush out of his way. "You already are!" He grinned at Philip, then turned back to the trail. "Cook tells me you're the best speller in Tathenland. That's topping good."

"That's not . . ." Philip sighed. "Thank you." They continued walking.

Late in the afternoon, Adam felt that they were getting closer to Snowcap. But he was also confused. He stooped to examine a particularly trampled-upon bit of trail. "It appears she's hoofin' it, not ridin' Peat." He looked closer. "Odd."

Philip didn't see anything wrong with walking; it seemed a wise choice when traveling with a dangerous horse. "Why odd?"

"It's not odd to walk, really. Peat's not too dab in the forest, and p'rhaps Snowcap's tryin' not to tire him out too much. Here's the odd part: there are two sets of footprints, both the kid's size. One with boots, one with soft shoes—moccasins? But who's she scampering with?"

"You mean someone her own age? That's not possible. She doesn't have any friends. And no one else has gone missing. And who wears moccasins?"

Adam began walking again, briskly. "Exactly. Well,

one benefit of her footin' it is we can likely snabble her tonight. Then we can find out what she's up to and how to help her."

"Adam?"

"What?"

"The pups?" They seemed louder to Philip.

"They're still far away—" But then Adam cocked his head and furrowed his brow, listening. "No, you're right, they're closer. So—let's rattle, eh?"

They followed the trail as quickly as they could walk. But as the moments passed, the pups grew louder and louder. Finally, the creatures were so close that Philip could hear them panting. He could hear sticks breaking. "What shall we do?"

Adam, still jogging ahead, said, "Find ourselves a bolt-hole." He slowed down to wait for Philip.

"I've heard they'll attack anything alive. That's what I've heard!" Philip shrieked.

The yelps grew suddenly high-pitched and excited, as if the pups smelled prey. "We'll work on that notion, then," Adam said. "Climb."

"What?" Philip looked up. The tree above him divided into solid, wide branches, beginning about six feet off the ground.

"Shake your shambles, man. We haven't got all day." Adam shoved Philip up. And followed just in time.

From the lower branches, they peered down and saw a pack of six pups race into view, led by a brown-and-gray-spotted one slightly bigger than the others, about the size of a possum. The rest were the size of water rats; they'd have looked very much like rats if they didn't have furry tails and stout, powerful legs. These were not cuddly, playful, and affectionate puppies. They were tiny, deadly, wild dogs with knife-sharp teeth, snapping jaws, beady eyes, long claws, and the temperaments of killers.

Philip and Adam stared down in horrified fascination as the pups surrounded the tree. Soon more joined the pack, until several dozen milled around on the ground below. (Clinging to the trunk, Philip counted thirty-two pups, but he couldn't be sure because they kept moving.) Adam yelled down and threw pieces of bark, but this seemed only to make them angrier, so he stopped.

The throng showed no sign of leaving. They kept howling and barking, watching the men. After an interminable hour, Adam said to Philip, "Better get cozy. We could be here awhile."

"How—how long?"

"Depends how much they want to eat us." He studied the pups. "They look mighty hungry."

The afternoon wound down. Adam took the pack off his back and stowed it in the tree. He gave Philip a piece of rope so that he could secure himself to the branch. Philip's grip had gone white, but after he knotted one end of the rope around his waist and the other around his branch, he relaxed a bit.

"What do we do now?" he asked.

"We wait."

31

NIGHT SINGING

Lucy and Snowcap moved through the woods all day.
While they traveled, Snowcap told Lucy about being unexpectedly followed from the stables. Who had followed her? It couldn't have been Markham and Renard, since they had followed Lucy. At any rate, Snowcap was quite certain that she had lost whoever it was. However, Markham and Renard would certainly have discovered by morning—if not earlier—that Peat was missing, and they might right now be trailing the girls into the woods. Surely someone in the village had heard Peat galloping toward the wall and would tell about it; it was only a matter of time. Lucy and Snowcap assumed the worst

and tried to make as much progress as possible before nightfall.

"Don't worry. They won't catch us," said Snowcap to make Lucy feel better for being a little slow. "They'll be walking, too."

"Not riding horses?"

"The horses are scared of Renard."

Carrying Rob was tiring for Lucy. And he seemed less content; his sleep, though almost constant, was restless. When he woke, he wanted only to eat and go back to sleep again, and even while he ate, he never seemed to wake fully—his eyes glazed as if they saw dreams. Lucy wondered if Rob were trying to escape the woods by sleeping through them. *Or is the curse coming back somehow?* she couldn't help but worry. She walked faster to stop herself from thinking.

They had heard the pups in the distance all day but had not seen any of them, though late in the afternoon they came across the skeleton of a possum. It was picked clean, and its broken bones gleamed as white as alabaster in the shadows of the woods. Stooping to look, Snowcap saw small toothmarks in the bones—gnawing marks—and scuffled prints in the leaves where the pups had jostled for food.

After coming across the possum bones, they walked about an hour southwest before they stopped to build camp. Lucy immediately set a fire and boiled walnuts; she wanted to make enough mash to last another day or two while they traveled. As she fed Rob, she rested her aching right hand on his warm forehead. Snowcap hadn't asked about the hand. Lucy was proud of herself for hiding the pain well. *It doesn't help to show your weaknesses to your enemy*, she thought, hesitating briefly over the last word.

While Lucy was feeding Rob, Snowcap gathered more wood for the fire and brought out the last of her own food: turnips and onions and one scraggly carrot.

"I'll take care of those," said Lucy.

"Thank you." Snowcap tried to hide her relief at not having to cook her miserable stew again.

"You'd just burn them," Lucy added. Then, a bit sorry for her rudeness, she said in a slightly softer tone, "You have to stir through to the bottom as it cooks. And use more water, and don't cook it quite so long. That's all." She laid Rob down on his blanket and began to put the vegetables in the pot, along with a handful of dried seaweed and some dried fish from her bundle.

As Lucy prepared the stew and Snowcap dozed against a tree, the sky grew dark and Rob awoke. Realizing he was no longer being carried, he fussed wearily. Lucy said, "He wants to be held."

Snowcap opened her eyes and looked at Lucy, who was still stirring the pot. "Do you want me to do it?" She meant her words to sound like an offer, but she was groggy and they didn't come out quick enough.

"Use your judgment," Lucy snapped. "There's a baby crying, but don't put yourself out."

Snowcap's temper flared. "Well then, I won't." And she sat, unmoving, though she eyed Rob worriedly.

Rob began to cry louder. Lucy gritted her teeth. "Will you hold him until I've got our supper made?"

Snowcap smiled as if she'd won a wager. "Of course. How nice of you to ask." She walked to the blanket, sat down cross-legged, picked Rob up, and put him on her lap. He quieted instantly, and she said to him in her softest tones, "Oh, do you like me? You're certainly not like your sister, then, are you?" Ignoring Lucy, she murmured to Rob, telling him what a sweet baby he was and how different he was from his sister in every way. Rob waved his hands.

"What do you want?" Snowcap asked him. "A story? I can't think of any stories right now. How about a song?" She considered, but she couldn't think of any song that seemed right for Rob—that seemed right to be sung here, in the woods, on the run.

Snowcap's nurse had sung to her when she was a baby; her mother had sung to her almost every night before she went to bed; she had sung in church services and gone Christmas caroling and sung birthday songs to her parents. But most of this singing ended when they died. Curiously, the only two songs she could think of now were from strange sources: one was a song that Adam had taught her, a song that prisoners sang on the boats to America; and the other was a song that she had heard only once in her life, a couple of months ago in midspring, when she had ridden Peat out into a big meadow at the southern end of Baytown. They had ridden very fast; Snowcap had decided they should stop and rest. She was lying flat on her back with the tall grasses waving above her, while Peat grazed down at the stream, when she overheard a man singing. Lonesome and slightly whiny, the man's song wandered up and down the tune as if it couldn't quite find the proper trail. Snowcap hadn't known who the singer was, but the voice sounded familiar. She had continued listening, dozing in the sunshine, the voice like a dream. She felt as if the song pinned her to the grass, to the land. But she was warm and cozy in the sunshine, so she didn't mind.

Now she remembered this song with utter clarity, not the fuzzy way that one usually remembers dreams. She was sure that she remembered both of the songs perfectly, the first exactly as Adam had taught it and the second exactly as the unseen man had sung it. So she sang. First Adam's song; it was the more jouncy of the two. That is, the *tune* was more jouncy, though the words were quite mournful. But Rob wouldn't understand the words anyway, she reasoned, so they didn't matter.

Snowcap sang:

Oh England, sweet England,
I know I'll ne'er see your shore;
If I do it's a stone in my heart.
And my fingers are frozen, and my feet they are sore.
I wander the woods and knock at death's door.
But if I can just live
For twelve years more,
I will soon say hello to Virginny.

Now that she was singing it, a few of the words seemed wrong. But that couldn't be helped—songs had a way of changing when they were sung by different singers. *Just like stories*, she thought. And Rob was calm and blinked up at her sleepily. Even if he had been older, he wouldn't have understood the words, for the song was in English, not Colay. So words truly didn't matter. Snowcap moved on to the song she had heard in the field:

You are the treasure I hope to find;
I've looked so far away;

To find my heart's true joy I'll look
At the end of the farthest day.

Where you are I do not know
And whether bound or free,
Whether sleeping on unmapped islands,
Or sunk in the darkling sea.

Treasure! Pleasure!
From India to Araby—
Chase you! Face you!
From old London to wild Virginny—
On land, in sky, or sea.
I call you right home to me.

As she sang, she once again wondered who the singer in the meadow had been and from where the song had come. Somehow the words were melding with a song her mother had taught her. They weren't quite right anymore. But her audience was not bothered by any changes she might inadvertently have made. In her arms, Rob fell into a dreamless baby slumber, unconcerned about pups or curses or trackers in the night. Snowcap kept singing the songs over and over, weaving them together, until they finally became one song: about a treasure buried somewhere between Virginia and India; lost somewhere among sea and land and sky; searched for by a prisoner with stiff hands, sore feet, and indestructible determination.

Lucy continued to stir the stew, never stopping, until it was done.

32

WILD PUPS

The girls ate silently. Lucy was jealous of how easily Snowcap had struck up a friendship with Rob. After all, Lucy was the one who had rescued him. And she was Rob's sister; Snowcap was no one to him. And now here Snowcap was, singing Anglish songs to him, songs Lucy couldn't even understand. It wasn't fair. Lucy felt as if Rob had betrayed her.

Snowcap, meanwhile, suspected that Lucy didn't like her singing, and this made her angry. She was one of the best singers in Tathenn! Hadn't the choirmaster told her so time and time again? What right did a Colay girl have to turn up her nose at the Child Governor's singing?

So dinner was a rather silent affair. The conversation proceeded as follows:

Snowcap: "I hear the pups."

Lucy: *(no response)*

Snowcap: "I hope they come here. I'd like to see them."

Lucy, in a freezing tone: "You *would* wish something like that."

After dinner, Snowcap stalked away toward Peat. Lucy scowled at the dirty pot. "Don't worry about cleaning up, your lordship," she called after Snowcap. "The Colay girl will take care of it."

Snowcap burned. Such rudeness! She leapt on Peat's back and raced toward the fire, swerving at the last minute to reach down off the horse and snatch up the pot, which she threw as far as she could into the woods. Then she and Peat disappeared into the forest, hooves pounding as Lucy glared after her.

Snowcap and Peat ran. She was angry, but not too angry to think about Peat's well-being, so she relaxed her hold, and he soon slowed down. They were headed east. Snowcap knew she needed to head back to camp–she didn't intend to break her promise and have that girl remind her of it all her life–but she wanted to scare Lucy a bit first. So she wouldn't go back *quite* yet.

Then she heard the pups again. Now, they sounded nearer; she was headed toward them. There seemed to be a large pack. Here was an adventure! Lucy was afraid of the pups and believed all kinds of silly things about them, but Snowcap Margaret O'Kelly would prove that *she* wasn't afraid; she would conquer them and maybe even capture one to show Lucy how brave she was. First, she would investigate the area, then she would attack. But even as Snowcap looked forward to a fight, she felt a yearning to see the pups. Their voices sounded so full of longing. She gave herself a shake; dismounted; found a stout stick; and remounted, carrying her weapon. Nudging Peat, who never balked, she rode in the direction of the pups.

When they reached the clearing where the pups were gathered, Snowcap and Peat moved as silently as a medium-sized horse could. The pups were making so much noise that they didn't notice anyone approaching. Snowcap, still seated on Peat's back, leaned forward and peeped out into the clearing. The pups were pressed against one of the trees, looking up into its branches and howling. Snowcap squinted, but though the night was bright, she could not make out what kind of animal they had treed. She settled down to wait and see what would happen, stroking Peat's mane to keep him still.

Presently, she heard a thin, trembling voice say, "Perhaps singing would help. I've heard that singing to animals calms them."

"Good idea. Why don't you try it?" a second voice answered steadily.

The first man began to sing:

"*You are the treasure I hope to find–*" and then broke off. "I'm afraid I can't do it. *I'm* not calm enough myself. How do *you* keep from being scared?"

"I don't," Adam replied (for, Snowcap quickly realized, it was Adam's steady voice, and Philip who had been trying to sing. *Her* song. She tucked that thought away for later). "I just know that right now we're safe, and there's nothing I can change by worrying. More bread?"

"No, thank you."

And they were silent. Snowcap waited, thinking.

Then she realized that the pups were pressing even closer around the tree, and they appeared to be gnawing at it. She twisted the big stick in her hands. The pups were chewing and clawing the tree down! They had bitten and clawed through the bark in a ring and were now tearing away at the trunk, like crazed water rats with talons. Something had to be done, and soon, or they would fell the tree with Adam and Philip still in it. And yet—she felt almost as much concern for the pups as for the men. The animals didn't know what they were doing. She was sure of it.

Without thinking any further, Snowcap urged Peat into a run, and they raced into the clearing. At the top of her lungs, she shouted, "Avaunt! Begone!" (words from one of her mother's fairy stories that seemed appropriate now).

Philip yelped, "What's that?" and Adam said, in happy surprise, "Snowcap!"

Snowcap raised her stick high; nevertheless, she never struck a blow. The brown-and-gray leader stood his ground, near the tree, and Snowcap could see that he had only one eye and a badly scarred face. Peat ran as if to trample him, but just in time, Snowcap screamed, "No!" and horse and rider swerved. The lead pup jumped back with a yip and ran into the woods. The remainder of the pack scattered after him.

Suddenly the clearing was empty, and the woods were silent. Snowcap felt an inexplicable sense of loss. And then she remembered that she'd just saved two men.

Philip fell from his branch and, caught by the rope

around his waist, dangled inelegantly. He swung for a moment and then, as the rope gave way, crashed to the ground. When he opened his eyes, two faces loomed over him. "Gosh," he said weakly.

33

In Which We Hear a True Story of Love and Adventure

After Philip caught his breath, the men followed Snowcap back to camp. (She had neglected to mark her trail, but fortunately Peat remembered the way.) At camp, they found Lucy sitting with Rob on her lap, singing to him in Colay, low and off-key. She stopped when she saw them and jumped up as if ready to run off.

"Everything's fine," said Snowcap. "They're my friends. They're here to help. And they have news." Snowcap motioned for them to sit down. "This is Adam. And Philip." She turned to the men. "This is Lucy. And Rob."

Adam smiled and spoke in almost perfect Colay: "Pleased."

"Charmed," said Philip in clumsy Colay that sounded a lot like English. (Snowcap's father had decreed that learning Colay was important—something about how the English aristocrats should have studied Gaelic, whatever that meant. Yet despite Philip's attempts to learn Colay, his pronunciation left much to be desired.)

Lucy turned to Snowcap. "What's happening?"

Snowcap grinned, their argument forgotten. "I rescued them!"

"Actually," Philip said, "I think her horse rescued us. We were trapped by the pups, and Peat chased them off."

"That's why the pups haven't been bothering us," Snowcap broke in. "They're scared of Peat."

"That's my theory," said Philip. "I understand there aren't any such large animals in the forest."

"That's true." Lucy nodded her head thoughtfully. If Peat were protecting them from the pups, then she really needed to continue traveling with Snowcap.

"I don't know about that," said Adam. "I rode Acorn out into the woods, not five years ago—Peat's mother," he informed Philip.

Philip nodded, thinking how much easier Adam was to understand in Colay than in English—if that was indeed what he usually spoke.

Adam continued. "Well, I didn't get more than a half hour out when I heard pups coming. They chased me, and it was a good thing that Acorn could clear the wall, let me tell you. They were after her."

"But what else could it be?" said Snowcap. "They really seemed frightened of Peat."

"You looked pretty frightening yourself, Snowcap." Adam cheerily sat down before the dying embers of the fire. "What say we catch each other up on the rest of the news?" He glanced at Lucy. "Perhaps you might begin, miss. We didn't even know you were part of this adventure."

Lucy watched as Adam took a stick, stirred the embers, and added wood. "I'd rather hear your story first," she said.

Snowcap snorted loudly. "She's so stubborn; there's no reasoning with her."

Philip and Adam exchanged a look, and Adam murmured, "Oh? That's some justice."

Snowcap frowned and went on. "I might as well begin with my story." As they sat around the kindling fire, she recounted what she'd heard in the cellar—about the plan to kill her and to frame Adam—and how she had run away and come back for Peat. "What did they mean about framing the Colay *again*?"

"I could guess," Adam said.

Lucy put Rob back down on her lap. "No guessing needed. I can tell you." She held out her left hand, palm up and open, just as Amarrah had done when she began this story. The right hand she kept folded stiffly in her lap. "The Colay did not kill Governor O'Kelly and his wife. It was a scheme by a man named Mark the Ham."

"Oh, my," said Philip.

"Mark the Ham stole power. From the Governor and from the Colay. Because of him, the Colay lost all the influence we ever had with the Anglish."

"And that's why they were poisoning my oatmeal," Snowcap muttered. "So he could rule."

Philip jerked. "*Poison?*"

Adam looked worried. "Why didn't you tell me? Or Philip?"

Snowcap glanced away, as if the dark shrubbery were suddenly very interesting. "I didn't think—that is—"

"We *care* about you, you idiot," said Adam. "Next time someone tries to kill you, *ask for help.*" He glared.

Still studying the foliage, Snowcap gave a short nod.

Lucy watched the exchange uncomfortably, remembering Amarrah's similar words to her.

Adam turned to Lucy. "But how did Markham kill the O'Kellys?"

"The person who told me the story didn't know," said Lucy.

"Who told you?" asked Adam. "I want to talk with this man."

"It was the Lady who lives on the Gray Mountain."

Snowcap didn't say anything. She now stared at the fire, which was still struggling to light.

Adam fussed with the twigs. "Hmm," he said, after a moment. "If Markham did it, then Renard was behind it."

"Renard?" asked Lucy.

"The steward. He's the one really in charge. Just without the title."

The truth flashed on Lucy. *A man with power but no title.* "The small man!" She gaped. "Curved like a heron."

"That's him," said Adam.

Snowcap looked up. "Yes, the man who chased you. You've met him before?"

"No," said Lucy. "Not really."

"Then what—?"

"There's something more," said Lucy. "This Renard . . ."

Snowcap leaned toward her.

". . . told my father he had magic. Renard said he could make things happen. And then—"

"Then what?" echoed Philip.

"Then all the men and boys froze into statues. All except this baby."

Everyone gaped now.

"You are speaking in metaphor, yes?" asked Philip.

"I'm speaking real. This Renard made bad things happen."

Philip could believe that. But how had no one seen it happen? "I thought . . . he just banned the Colay from Tathenn. We didn't see them anymore. . . . I didn't know. . . ."

"What were they fighting over? Renard and your father?" asked Adam.

"The rocks. The ground. Power."

The wood Adam had added to the fire finally caught, and the flames leapt up. There was a long silence.

Lucy waited for Snowcap to bring up the story she'd overheard that first night: the prophecy about how Rob was meant to save the Colay. But Snowcap didn't speak. *Maybe she does have some decency in her,* Lucy thought. *Or maybe she's just saving that story for the right time.*

Philip cleared his throat. "Why didn't we know any of this earlier? That the men are turned to—to stone?"

"We could have, sure," said Adam. "My grammy always said"—he switched here to English—"*You can only surtoute the flash-cove you want to snabble.*"

Philip stared. "What in the world does that mean?"

Adam spoke again in Colay. "We only know what we want to know. The horse we've bet on."

"That's not true," said Snowcap. "I always know—" She stopped and looked down, confused. She had been blind to so many things.

"There's something I'd like to know," Lucy said hesitantly, looking into the faces flickering in the fire's light. "That is—what were Robert and Nora O'Kelly like?" She shifted Rob, who was sleeping, more snugly into her lap. "Were they well loved? Good?"

Snowcap's head shot up. "Of course they were! Are you saying that my parents were bad rulers?" Her eyes blazed. Here was something she was sure of.

Adam shook his head. "Lucy's not saying that at all. She never met your parents, so she wants to know what they were like."

Snowcap lowered her head again.

Philip turned to Lucy. "Governor O'Kelly was kind and wise and noble, as was his wife. In their time, food was plentiful and learning at its golden height—"

Adam broke in. "They were good leaders. Good as their time. But not perfect." He poked the logs and sparks flew up. "Want me to tell you how they came over here?"

"Please," said Lucy. Snowcap lifted her eyes to watch Adam.

"Snowcap's heard this story many times. But I think she'll not object to hearing it again." Snowcap shook her head quickly, and Adam continued: "Mr. and Mrs. O'Kelly came from Ireland to London to work in the household of Lord Clonbrony, whose only desire in life was to gamble. In time, the lord lost his entire estate and turned his servants out on the street, in a land where they could barely speak the language—theirs being Gaelic, not English. These poor souls had to find a way to make a living, and if they were lucky, they'd earn enough to get back to Ireland. But not many Londoners wanted to hire servants who spoke little English. Mr. O'Kelly couldn't find work, all their money ran out, and they had nothing to eat. Mrs. O'Kelly was sickly-like and needed food."

"Was she pregnant?" Lucy asked.

Philip looked astounded at such an indelicate question, but Adam smiled and continued: "I believe she was. One day, they were so desperate that Mr. O'Kelly stole a loaf of bread. The next day, still unable to find work, he stole an apple. The next, a pail of milk. On that day, he was caught and gaoled in Newgate. London gaols are bad places, and many die in them. Fortunately for him, Mr. O'Kelly's trial came early, so he didn't have to linger long in Newgate. But the judge sentenced him to be transported to America. This was a terrible sentence; he would not see his unborn child for seven years.

"His wife thought of a way to keep her family together. The day after his sentence, she walked into a tavern and stole a silver spoon."

"The Bear's Arms," said Snowcap.

"So it was"–Adam nodded–"and the owner had an eagle eye for thieves. Nora also was clapped into Newgate. She came up before the same judge and received the same sentence: transportation to America."

"She wanted this?" said Lucy doubtfully.

"Of course," said Snowcap. "To keep them together."

"It was risky," admitted Adam, "for she might not've been sentenced to transportation at all, or she might've been sent to a different part of the colonies. But the

O'Kellys were lucky for once: they were placed not only on the same voyage but on the same boat, where they sat next to each other in the ship's hold. I sat with them, and they told me this tale. Robert O'Kelly was proud of his clever wife. And Nora O'Kelly was proud of her daring husband."

Adam looked around the circle. "This is what they were like, and they brought their love to their new home. They wanted to make this a home for us all." He paused and then said to Lucy, "Though I don't think they considered enough what you Colay wanted. They thought mostly of the English."

"They thought of themselves!" Snowcap exclaimed. "They had to. They had found a new world!"

"New," Lucy muttered.

"And a fine job they did," said Adam soothingly. "All I say is that they might've thought more of others who suffered as they once had."

"This was where they went wrong," said Lucy.

Where they went wrong? Snowcap felt as if Lucy and Adam were speaking a language she didn't know, yet somehow they seemed to understand each other. Philip looked just as puzzled.

Adam cocked his head. "But—there's more to it. The wrong that led to their deaths was too much trust that all people were like them. They believed the Colay would become like the English, but also that the English were all the same—all like them—criminals due to circumstance. They didn't believe any of us would commit crimes here in Tathenland."

"Yet here we all are," murmured Philip, looking around the group.

"That's not really what I meant," said Adam.

"Adam's right," said Lucy. "Running away, stealing a horse—"

"—and food, and rope," added Philip.

"—that's all crimes of circumstance. The O'Kellys' murderers committed crimes of the heart," finished Adam.

Philip wanted to change the topic to something he actually understood. Not *Wrongs* or *Crimes* or *Trust*. He felt he no longer understood these words, or perhaps he had never understood them. Turning to Lucy, who was watching Rob sleep, he said, in his best teacherly voice, "I'm curious where you are from."

"I'm from Sunset," Lucy answered.

Once again Philip felt bewildered. "Where?"

"Dover," said Adam.

"Oh." Philip sighed.

Now Lucy looked confused.

"That's what the English call your island," explained Adam. "Renard named it that when we arrived. The name kind of stuck. The Gray Lady lives there?"

"Yes." With her left hand, Lucy sketched a rough map in the dirt. "Not in the village, but in her own hut, partway up the mountain in the middle of the island. That's where you can find her. It's a beautiful place."

Adam bent over the map. "Sounds lovely. I'd like to see your island someday, Lucy." He smiled at her. "And meet your family and friends."

"I don't have friends," said Lucy.

"Why not?"

Lucy pulled back her hair, and the handprint glowed red in the firelight.

"Brilliant," said Adam. "Lit from within."

Startled, Lucy dropped her hair, and it covered her face again, like a curtain pulled over a tapestry.

Adam leaned back on his hands. "I really *would* like to visit your island."

"But"—Snowcap suddenly rejoined the conversation—"I hear nothing ever happens on Dover."

"Sunset," said Lucy.

"Whatever its name is. It must be a small, dull place."

Lucy refused to give Snowcap the satisfaction of getting her angry. So she said, evenly, "A lot of things happen there."

Adam noted, "Tathenn is pretty small, too, in the whole scheme of things."

"Much smaller than England," Philip agreed.

"England is immense," said Snowcap, eyeing Lucy closely. "And beautiful."

"It's a good place to be from," said Philip.

"It *is* a good place. So's Ireland. But so's this." Adam stretched. "We're all deep tired. What say we sleep now, and talk more in the morning?"

They all unrolled their blankets and curled up near Peat around the embers of the fire. But Rob was the only one who slept deeply; he'd been sinking into a heavier and heavier sleep as the evening progressed.

Lucy's sore hand felt like awls were poking it, and rubbing it didn't help. Without knowing exactly why, she took the lifestone out of her pouch and laid her hand on top of it. The stone felt warm and solid as she drifted to uneasy sleep.

Adam lay for a long time staring into the darkness. *Renard. Statues. Gray Lady.* More answers, more questions.

Philip also lay awake, listening to the night noises and Peat's heavy breathing. He thought about the story Adam had told. It was no secret how the O'Kellys had been arrested in England; people retold the story all over Baytown. Everyone knew the stories of one another's crimes. Yet in his writings, Philip had not been honest about himself or the O'Kellys. In dressing up history on paper, he had misrepresented it—no, *distorted* it, beyond recognition. Adam's telling, on the other hand, was pretty much true. And Philip realized that Adam's version was best: not only true, but also the most interesting. It was a story of true love, a story of adventure, a story fit for people old and young. It was the story that Philip should have written.

Snowcap woke in the darkest part of the night, certain she was being pursued by someone in a long, hooded black cloak. As she was running, she realized that it was her own cloak that was chasing her, and that she herself was in the cloak, or maybe it was Lucy—or was it Adam? She couldn't tell for certain. She woke with a gasp. Rob shifted in his sleep, and she reached over to him and stroked his cheek. Lucy, lying curled on the other side of Rob, frowned without opening her eyes. Snowcap slid her hand away. Near morning, she fell back asleep.

34

A Girl May Smile and Smile, and Yet Be Jealous

First thing the next morning, Snowcap confronted Adam. "What do you think you are doing?"

"Scrubbin' up before yamming my breakfast."

"No. With Lucy. Why are you being so nice to her?"

Adam dunked his entire head in the stream and came up blowing. "Whew! That's cold!"

"Answer me!"

"What kind of a question is it? I'm bein' nice to her because she's a person and she deserves it." He wiped off his face with his shirtfront and wrung out his hair.

Snowcap felt—she didn't know the word for how she felt, but she knew it wasn't a good feeling. And she didn't know what to do about it, so she launched into teasing. "Ooooh. I think you *like* her. Are you going to *marry* her? Ha! It's despicable–so far beneath you."

"I'm a grown-up ragamuffin. No one's beneath me."

"Well, it's disgusting. You're a cheap–"

"Snowcap." Adam interrupted firmly. "I'm not interested in gettin' manacled to anyone, but in a few years, when Lucy's grown up some, she might be–a wonderful person to know. At any rate, I'm glad already to have met her, and you should be, too." He pulled his hair back into its customary pigtail, then took Snowcap's shoulders. "None of us is perfect, or we wouldn't be here, eh? But–by my grammy's good name, kid! Be a first-rate kind of imperfect. An interesting kind."

"You think I'm dull?" Snowcap's head felt like it were going to explode. Her hands curled into fists.

"No. But predictable. For instance, when I saw you comin' just now, I knew you'd be yelpin'. And next, you're thinkin' of how hard to pummel me and of nasty things to say about my kin. Right?"

Snowcap punched him, called his mother a ferret, and ran off. Later, alone in the woods, she cried–something Adam would not have predicted.

35

TOWARD THE
NAKED MOUNTAIN

That morning, they lingered over their camp. Lucy knew they needed to move on, but Snowcap was nowhere to be found. Rob barely opened his eyes when Lucy changed him. In her heart, she feared the worst. She stroked his cheek to wake him for his feeding, but he wouldn't rouse. She reached inside his swaddling and felt his left foot: cool, as always. Maybe a little cooler.

For the first time since she took Rob up the Gray Mountain, Lucy despaired, but she bit her lip hard and managed not to cry. Wrapping her good hand around her luck pouch and the lifestone inside, she wished for Rob to wake up—and she wished she hadn't thrown away all her luck. Then she called Adam and Philip. Philip blew in Rob's face and sang to him, until Lucy snapped, "Stop it. You're not helping at all. He won't wake up."

Philip wrung his hands. Adam looked grave. "I don't know much about babies," he said, "but you need to get him help as soon as possible."

"He's *not* turning to stone," Lucy said firmly, hoping she could change the truth with her words. "It's something else."

"Whatever might be causing it," said Adam, "we should get him out of these woods."

Lucy nodded. "We need to get to the desert. Now." At that moment, Snowcap returned. Lucy ignored her. "Let me pack up Rob's breakfast, and I'll be ready to go."

Adam murmured the story to Snowcap, who said, "Did you try to jiggle him?"

"Do you know *anything* about babies?" Lucy asked, slamming the pot to the ground. "You don't jiggle them."

"Are you sure the desert's the place to go? Maybe your home would be better," said Adam. "What did that Gray Lady say?"

Lucy gritted her teeth to squelch her panic. "She said the desert is our best hope."

"I've never been there," Philip said. "But I'd guess that it would take a few days at least."

"That much time seems like a big risk with a sick child. Unless . . ."–Adam paused–"unless you want to travel faster than walking." He looked at Peat, who was munching grass nearby.

Snowcap's eyes darted from Adam to Peat to Lucy. "No!" She turned back to Adam. "Peat's mine! I rescued him so that he could be with *me*."

"Technically," Philip said, "Lucy rescued Peat as much as you did."

"But Peat won't let anyone ride him except me! He won't!"

"I doubt that's true," said Adam gently.

"He's big. . . ." Lucy walked toward Peat, with Rob in her arms. She hoisted her pack onto his back and stood next to him, staring at Snowcap.

"Sure," said Adam. "He's big enough for two to ride. Two *and* a baby."

"Oh." Snowcap felt foolish. They weren't suggesting that she give Peat away, but that she go along. She tried to cover her mistake. "We'll both ride Peat; we'll get to the desert as fast as we can."

Lucy smirked. "What a kind offer." She turned to Philip and Adam. "Would you do something for me? Will you go to the Lady on the Gray Mountain and tell her that you've seen me? She will be glad of the news. And so will my mother."

Adam nodded. "We'll go there as soon as we can. But first we'll follow you to the edge of the woods and see you off into the desert."

Philip opened his mouth to protest, then shut it.

"Thank you." Lucy turned to Snowcap. "Let's go. We don't have time to waste." She handed Rob, still sleeping, to Adam. Snowcap gathered her things and tied her pack on top of Lucy's. Then she climbed on Peat's back. She pulled Lucy up behind her; then Adam gave Rob back to Lucy, who tied him into a blanket around her chest. After they were arranged, the girls left camp on horseback, traveling briskly westward.

✤ ✤ ✤

For the first hour or so, they moved in utter silence, until Snowcap couldn't stand it anymore. Why didn't Lucy talk? Even fighting was better than this quiet. Perhaps she could make up with Lucy, and then they could talk again. Perhaps they could even entertain each other. That could help take their minds off of Rob, lying like a rock between them.

"I'll tell you a story," Snowcap began. "It's only fair, after your story last night—about my parents and the Rebellion." She felt as though she were offering sweets. "I'll tell you how the English arrived here. It's one of my favorites. My father used to tell it to me all the time."

"That's all the story you can tell? I already know how you came here. I've heard it a hundred times. You came in big ships, and sailed into the harbor at Picle, and you took our land and wouldn't leave."

"That's not it at all!" Snowcap protested, swiveling her head to look back at Lucy. "Our ships sank," she said, turning forward again. "The English were prisoners, chained in the ships, and the Colay helped free them and bring them to shore. The English were not conquerors; they were convicts." She paused, then said slowly, "You're right about one thing: we did take your land. But what can we do about that now? This is our home. I was born here."

"I just wish you would leave," Lucy said quietly.

The girls rode onward. Snowcap wished she could have told the story better. Lucy wished the story had a better ending. Both were silent again.

After another two hours, the undergrowth began to

grow more dense; Peat was having a hard time picking his way through. "Maybe it would be better if we went north and then worked our way west along the coast," said Snowcap. "We'll lose a bit of time, but once we get to the coast, we can travel a lot faster."

Lucy couldn't help but agree. "I don't think it's more than an hour away," she said. "I can smell the sea."

They turned and headed north.

Adam and Philip walked in the wake of the girls, trailing behind them through the woods. They heard no pups; Philip thought that the creatures, still terrified of Peat, must have retreated to another part of the forest. After several hours of following the trail west, Adam stopped. "They've spun the wrong way. Here." The trail veered sharply to the north, toward the sea. "Where will this take them? D'you know?"

"Well," Philip said, glad to be asked, "I've never been out here, as you know, but I've constructed a map from my conversations with early explorers." Adam nodded impatiently. "We should be south of the Naked Mountain. I think they are headed for Botanist's Bay."

"I've heard it's a riffraff place."

"By all accounts it's a *strange* place. The Colay call it the Bay of Oddities, because odd things happen there—people disappear and sometimes reappear; strange creatures inhabit the sea; boats go astray—and *we* call it Botanist's Bay, because if there had been a botanist aboard our ships, he would have wanted to study the wildlife there."

"Hmm. Maybe they'll hoof up the mountain instead." Adam did not sound very hopeful.

"Now that would be bad, from what I've heard. The Naked Mountain is a hard climb, almost completely bare. And it's a dead end. At the top, it drops into the sea in a steep cliff."

"Oh." Adam was distracted by something. He peered into the shrubbery.

Philip continued to lecture: "It's called the Cliff of Good Hope, and I heard—from Governor Robert O'Kelly, years ago—the Colay have a legend that if you are hopeful and pure of heart, good things can happen at that cliff. At any rate, it's a sheer drop-off into Botanist's Bay; so if our young ladies go there, they will have no choice but to turn around, and they'll lose hours of precious time." A branch broke in the distance ahead of them. "What is that noise?"

"I've been suspicioning about that for a while," said Adam, "but I can't see anything." He peered again through the shrubbery, which was particularly dense here. "Whatever it is, it's hustlin' away from us."

"Pups?" asked Philip nervously.

"I don't think so. We'd hear 'em yippin', wouldn't we?"

"Maybe we are close to the girls? We might be hearing them?"

"It's possible," said Adam. "Could also be we're not the only coves following Lucy and Snowcap."

Philip imagined Colay warriors surrounding them with spears and shuddered.

"Let's keep moving." Adam strode forward, following Peat's trail of broken branches toward the mountain.

Philip picked a burr out of his stockings and set off after Adam. They moved at a rapid pace, Philip hoping all the while that Snowcap and Lucy would have the sense to turn around. But he doubted Lucy knew the geography of the mainland well, and he was certain Snowcap didn't know anything about the woods west of Baytown.

Adam must have been thinking similar thoughts, for he asked, "Why isn't Snowcap in the know about the bay and the mountain? She's the Child Governor; she ought to know such things." He spoke over his shoulder without slowing his pace. "Come to think on it, we should all know, everyone who lives here. Why'd no one tell us about our own home? Why'd we not scout it out for ourselves?"

Philip stumbled and righted himself quickly. "I—no one thought it was necessary. No one goes there. To the mountain, I mean."

"Snowcap goes there—right this minute. Didn't she learn anything in your nib school?"

"Yes, I taught them European and English geography, and even a bit of Irish geography—for the O'Kellys' sake, you know."

"But not about Tathenn?"

"I—no."

"So she has no idea where she's headed?"

Philip drooped his head and trudged on. "Probably not."

Adam said in a gentler tone, "She might not've harked, anyway. You'll teach her somethin' useful, next time, hey? Meanwhile, let's find 'em and help 'em get back on the right trail." He shook his head at the tracks heading north and then stopped, so abruptly that Philip almost ran into him. Adam stooped to the ground, peering at something, and then he swore under his breath, a memorable phrase Philip hadn't heard since England.

Philip looked down. A small brass button. "Oh, no."

It was one of the few brass buttons that had come over from London, a prized possession—a button from Renard's coat. And it was lying in one of Peat's hoof-prints. Renard, and most probably Markham, were close on Lucy and Snowcap's trail.

"I don't understand," Philip said. "How did they know where to go? And how could they have followed so quickly?"

Adam twirled the button between his fingers. "I can guess they've been sniffin' after you and me. We haven't been careful about covering our tracks. And they jumped ahead of us when we stopped a few minutes ago. . . ." He squared his shoulders. "Let's shake our shambles! Come on!"

In their concern for Rob, both girls had forgotten about their pursuers in Baytown; they'd even forgotten that Adam and Philip were following them to the desert to make sure they were safe. They thought only of Rob, lying unmoving between them on the horse, tied to Lucy's chest. As Peat picked his way through the woods, both girls urgently felt the need to go faster, faster, for with each moment that Rob remained sleeping, they felt it would be harder and harder to wake him.

Neither girl had ever been so scared in her life. Lucy feared that her brother was freezing again, and that this time, there was nothing she could do to save him. Snowcap feared that she was losing the only person since her parents died who had not hated her, used or flattered her, or merely put up with her—Rob had actually seemed to like her.

The girls knew nothing about where they were headed except that they wanted to reach the coast, to move quicker and easier. They had only vague directions to find the desert philosophers: turn south at the desert and look for three low hills. They relied on Amarrah's assurance to Lucy that once they reached the desert, the philosophers would, somehow, find them.

After traveling for over an hour north, they still had not reached the sea. The trees were too tall to look beyond, and they did not know how much farther they had to go.

Lucy broke the silence. "Is there any way we can go faster?"

"Only by flying," said Snowcap. "Peat can't go any faster through such thick woods." She ducked a low-hanging branch, but its tendrils scratched her face as they went by. "I wish we *could* fly," she added.

"We'd have to be a lot lighter for that," said Lucy. "Even you," she noted dryly, swatting the same branch out of her way and barely managing to pass it without getting hit.

"Fine," said Snowcap testily. Her face stung with scratches. "I'll lighten my pack. Then I'll be able to fly."

"Hmm. Make sure you put down something really heavy. Like your temper," Lucy suggested.

"Funny." They jounced as Peat scrambled over some fallen branches and a menacing pile of gnawed squirrel bones. "So if this is our game, what will you put down? What would you give up in order to fly?"

"This is stupid," said Lucy.

"Do you have a better game?" Snowcap waited. "Then, play. Please," she added. Lucy still did not answer, and Snowcap began to feel angry again. "I know. You can put down your grouchiness."

"Fine," Lucy snapped. "If you put down your pride."

"If you put down your grudges."

Lucy laughed bitterly. "Really, your Highness, the heaviest thing you have is your horse. You couldn't fly away and carry him along, you know. Can you leave your only friend behind?"

Snowcap gasped; she could never leave Peat behind. "Well," she retorted, "your heaviest thing is your doubt. You don't really believe we can help Rob. Can you put that down? *Your* only true friend?"

They rode on. Snowcap could feel both Rob and Lucy stiff and silent behind her.

After a few moments, Lucy said, in a small voice, "I'll drop my burdens if you will."

Snowcap was tempted to snarl, to tell Lucy that the game *was* stupid and her answers were stupid, and she would *never* leave Peat behind, not even in a game, but then she felt Rob pressed like a hard little fist in her back. She knew she had to make up with Lucy—for Rob's sake—and she knew that for Rob's sake she *would* give up many things.

"Yes," Snowcap said quietly. "I will."

The trees thinned to nothing, and just ahead they saw a mountain rising smooth and naked. On the other side, they assumed, was the sea; gulls soared above and the waves' dull roar mingled with the birds' shrieks. "What shall we do?" asked Snowcap. Then she answered her own question: "Climb."

"We've come this far," said Lucy. "We'll reach the sea. I believe it."

They slid off Peat's back and began to climb.

36

HAWKS

The girls climbed the mountain on foot, Snowcap letting go of Peat's mane so that he could find his own path behind them, and Lucy carrying Rob in the sling across her chest. The baby still slept.

The girls scrambled over the rocks, crawling when the terrain was too steep to stand. Peat seemed to be having a much easier time than they were; every time Snowcap glanced back, he was climbing gamely along, occasionally pausing to eat tufts of grass that poked up through the rocks. *There was never a horse more sure-footed*, thought Snowcap.

Lucy didn't pay much attention to Peat, for she was

busy trying not to jar Rob every time she stumbled. After an intense half hour of climbing, Snowcap stopped to dig a stone out of her boot, and Lucy took advantage of the break to tighten the blanket around her shoulders; Rob was starting to bounce around. As she adjusted the sling, Lucy looked up to see how much farther it was—a long way! The mountain seemed to stretch past the sky, much higher than the Gray Mountain—and then she looked back to see how far they had come. They were actually making good progress. She could see all the way down to the tree line at the base of the mountain, and she threw a stone down just to see how far it would go. It skittered down the mountain until she lost sight of it and then, a second later, lost the sound of it as well. *A long way to fall*, Lucy thought, giving the sling one last tug.

Snowcap, having finished with one boot, pulled off the other. One lonely pebble rolled out of the second boot.

"Are you sure you can walk after such a boulder?" Lucy said. But her tone was friendly.

Snowcap responded in kind. "Thirsty?" She whistled for Peat, who ambled over. She dug out her water skin from her pack, and both girls drank.

Then Lucy glanced at Rob, unmoving on her chest, and started to say, "We'd better go." But halfway through, something in the corner of her vision moved.

At that same instant, Snowcap hissed, "Lucy! There! Did you see?" They were both looking at the same spot, down the mountain: at the tree line two shadows scurried behind a large boulder. One shadow was long and lean, the other, smaller and hunched.

"I'm going to guess," Lucy said, "that's not Philip and Adam."

"No," said Snowcap. "Let's go. Quickly."

They began to scramble, but as Lucy pointed out, there was nowhere to hide. ("That's obvious," began Snowcap, then she stopped herself.) The entire mountain was devoid of any plant life larger than a tuft of grass. Their only hope was to get over to the other side. Surely there they'd find trees in which they could lose Markham and Renard, or a slope down to the beach where they could mount Peat and ride away.

When the girls looked back, the pair was disappearing into another outcropping, farther up the mountain. Lucy and Snowcap began climbing even faster.

"What's at the top of the mountain, anyway?" asked Snowcap. "Will there be places to hide?"

"Don't know," Lucy grunted. "Haven't been here before."

"That's bad. On the other hand, I doubt that Markham and Renard know what's at the top, either. So I guess we're all riding the same horse."

When they were close to the top, Lucy stopped short.

"What now?" asked Snowcap.

"I just realized," said Lucy. "I've heard of this place. In a story."

"We don't have time for stories. Will it help us or not?"

"Don't know." Lucy started to climb again as she talked, puffing, Snowcap on her heels. "It was a winter fireside tale. About the tallest mountain in Tathenn. And how it ends in a high cliff to the sea. The cliff is so high, no one has ever climbed down and lived to tell about it."

"Oh. . . ." This time Snowcap stopped. She snatched up a rock and then smashed it to the ground, sending it clattering down the slope. "You might have thought of that earlier!"

Lucy glared back just long enough, then kept climbing. "I didn't know this was the mountain, did I? And I don't know if the story is true. It's kind of hard to believe."

"Why?"

"According to the story"—Lucy scrambled over a big rock—"once, when a maiden tried to escape from a ravisher—"

"A what?"

"A ravisher. That's what the story says. Don't interrupt." She paused, trying to think of the right words, the way it ought to be told. But most of the words wouldn't come back to her now. "The maiden ran here. There was no place to go. So she jumped."

"No, that's not helpful."

"*According* to the story"—Lucy huffed—"she turned into a butterfly. Because she was pure of heart. When she touched the earth, she became human again and returned to tell her village her tale."

"Still not helpful. Where's my knife?" Snowcap asked.

"In the pack somewhere. What are you doing?"

"If that story *is* true—if there's nowhere to go when we reach the top—we're going to fight."

At the top of the mountain, they could go no farther. The drop-off was sheer and steep, ending in the sullen, green bay far below. There was no way to climb down without falling. There was no way to fall down and survive. The girls stood on the stone precipice—a flat shelf of slate perched atop the mountain—and could not move.

Then they took a few steps back, away from the edge, and stared long and hard at the two shadows moving through a large rock pile not far below them.

Snowcap held her knife tightly in front of her, her other hand on Peat's neck. "Let them come," she growled.

"No!" Lucy said. And suddenly the answer came to her. "This is a place for hope, not for killing. They can still turn back. We need to talk to them, tell them to stop."

"Are you mad? They won't turn back. You don't know them."

"I *do* know them, from the stories I've heard. They *can* turn back." Lucy wasn't sure she believed what she was saying—and she couldn't even quite believe she was saying it—but there it was. For the first time in her life, she felt filled with hope. She opened her mouth, and the words that came out sounded like a tale. "No man is so evil that he cannot turn back. He always has the choice. A person can change." She faced the shadows where Markham and Renard hid, and the men materialized from the darkness. "Turn back!" Lucy called to them. "Turn back or our deaths will be on your heads! You can still turn back!" She reached into her luck pouch, pulled out the lifestone, and held it tightly in her right hand. It felt like it was pulsing.

Renard ignored Lucy. He called out in English, "Snowcap, child, you've been keeping low company.

Can't your little servant girl even speak a civilized language?"

"She's not my servant," Snowcap said in English and then switched back to Colay so that Lucy could understand. "She is telling you to turn back. As you well know, since you can speak Colay. Or are you so bad with languages that you've forgotten in a year?"

Renard laid his hand on Markham's shoulder and squeezed. "Oh, no, I remember," he said. "Just as I remember that the Colay are traitors and murderous wretches. Have you forgotten your parents so quickly, dear? What would they say about your new companion?"

"They'd think I was finally smart enough to see through your lies. Not a step closer!" Snowcap waved the knife and—Markham took a step back, away from the knife and out of Renard's grasp. But Renard didn't move.

"Go back," said Lucy. "There's still time to turn around." She was surprised at the calmness of her own voice, as if she were discussing net mending or goats.

Renard laughed—a quick, barking sound. "I'm afraid there *isn't* time to turn around. We have other plans."

Again Sir Markham stepped back, a very small step.

Lucy took a ragged breath. It wasn't working. Hopefulness wasn't working. Giving them the chance to do the right thing wasn't working. Lifestone in hand, she squatted down on the slate precipice and started writing the only Anglish spell she knew. Maybe the stone would understand and—what? Help her? But she didn't know what else to do, so she wrote.

Snowcap's eyes narrowed. "Who's in charge here, anyway? Is this your idea, *Mark the Ham*? Are you really going to do this?"

Renard answered, "We all know who's making the decisions here."

Snowcap waved her knife again. "Get away," she growled. "Or else."

"That's precious. Shall we show them our little surprise?" said Renard.

Markham nodded uncertainly, and it occurred to Snowcap that he hadn't spoken a word; that he had given up making decisions; that he wasn't, for all practical purposes, *there* anymore. Renard reached into his travel cloak and pulled out two stilettos, sharp and glinting in the sun. He held one out to Markham. Markham reached for it slowly, as if underwater.

"Ah." Snowcap stopped waving her knife, which now looked paltry. "So that's it."

"Yes," said Renard. "*That's* it. Oh, it will be very sad. That a Colay girl should kill the Child Governor, and then herself. But it will make for a good story, won't it?" He stepped closer, winding over the rock, Sir Markham wading behind.

"Wait!" said Snowcap. She grabbed Lucy's shoulder and tugged her upward from her scribbling. "Do something," she whispered. "Please."

Lucy jerked her shoulder loose and tucked her lifestone back into its pouch. Then she did something Snowcap did not expect: she started crying. No, not crying—sobbing (though Snowcap could see no tears). "Please," Lucy choked. "Please, sirs, let us say good-bye first. Let us say good-bye to the baby."

Renard kept climbing, but Sir Markham blinked, rubbed his beard, and finally spoke. "I suppose—I suppose it won't make any difference."

Renard stopped, stared at Markham for a moment, and said, "Fine. Of course." Then he tilted his head up at the girls. "Do be quick. We can't wait all day."

Lucy, taking Snowcap's hand, peered down at Rob, his face half hidden in the sling. "I just realized something, Rob," she said softly. "We don't need to be hopeful for them. We need to be hopeful for us."

"Are you almost done?" asked Renard.

"Just a moment," pleaded Snowcap. "We need a moment."

Lucy didn't look up, but she spoke a bit louder. "Remember," she said to Rob in a clear voice. "Remember to always be pure of heart and hopeful. Remember the ravisher and the maiden." At this, Snowcap sucked in her breath, but Lucy never glanced away from the baby. "Remember," she continued, "that wonderful things are sometimes possible if you truly believe in them."

"Ravisher?" said Renard sharply. "What is that in English? What are you saying?" He began to climb the last few rocks to reach the edge of the cliff. Markham trailed behind, stiletto dangling limply from his hand.

"Are you sure?" Snowcap asked Lucy. She squeezed Lucy's right hand, hard.

Lucy squeezed back. "I'm ready." Her aching hand tingled as if it were just on the verge of waking up. With her free hand she patted Rob, sleeping in the sling. "Let's go."

The afternoon light lit up Lucy's entire face, and Snowcap thought she had never seen anyone so beautiful. She gave Peat one last, longing pat on his neck. Then the girls stepped to the edge of the cliff and, still holding hands, stepped off.

✤ ✤ ✤

As Philip and Adam neared the top of the mountain, they saw the scene playing out above them. They could see the backs of Sir Markham and Renard, who were holding daggers, and Lucy and Snowcap beyond them, one standing and one squatting. Snowcap yelled, "Wait!" and Lucy stood up and said something they couldn't quite make out, and the girls talked to the baby for a moment. Adam whispered to Philip, "Come on." They began to creep up, still keeping their eyes on the events unfolding.

Which is when they saw the girls jump off the cliff.

Philip knew. In the split second before, he already knew. Markham and Renard were moving toward the girls. Adam was racing desperately for the cliff's edge. But Philip did nothing. It was too late.

Just as Markham and Renard reached the cliff, the girls were gone.

As the girls fell, Renard raised his dagger triumphantly, Sir Markham stood next to him and peered downward, Adam fell to his knees, and Philip watched from behind a large rock.

Then, from below the cliff's edge, two hawks rose. Glorious and wild they flew up from the very spot where the girls had vanished. So close that their wing tips brushed each other, they lifted in the breath of the deep sky.

As the hawks flew up, Renard slashed out with his stiletto as if to slice them from the air. He missed. And he fell against Markham, who flailed and grabbed Renard's coat for balance. Both men tried to right themselves,

Markham shouting "No!" and Renard shouting "Let go!" while slashing at Markham's hand still entangled in his cloak. Shrieking and writhing, the two men slid over the edge of the cliff.

And then they were gone. Their shrieks stopped. No birds flew up. No butterflies. No bats, no moths, no insects, no flying things—nothing.

Philip crawled out from his hiding spot, tapped Adam's shoulder tentatively, and they ran, carefully, to the lip of the cliff. Looking at the water far below, Adam and Philip saw—nothing—except two large stones (one tall and thin, one smaller and hunched), rosy pink alabaster in the sunshine, jutting out of the sea. On the far side of the bay, a winged dolphin (or something like it) humped above the water's surface, glittering emerald in the sun, and then disappeared. The bay was silent.

In white, jagged lettering on the stone ledge was Lucy's Anglish spell, the only one she knew, the one she had learned from her cousins so long ago: **NOT GIRLS**.

Philip and Adam looked up from the words, up into the sky. The two hawks floated on a current of air. The black hawk carried a small creature—a mouse?—in its beak and circled high as if eager to fly away, but the white hawk soared back toward them. It flew low over Peat, who raised his head and nickered. The white bird called twice, flying over Adam and Philip, and then the hawks soared up and away, west over the bay and toward the desert.

37

THE CLIFF OF GOOD HOPE

Adam sank slowly to his knees again. "We were so close!"

Philip, backing away from the edge and wishing that Adam would also take one giant step backward, understood something important for once in his life: "No. It was never up to us. They had to save themselves."

"By jumping?" Adam slammed his fist on the ground. "They should've—" And he stopped, dumbstruck, because there was nothing else, really, that the girls should have done.

Peat whinnied and moved a few steps away to find a clump of grass. Philip cleared his throat. "I think sometimes your only choice is not whether you will die—but how."

Adam turned once more to the cliff; Philip could not see his face. "So is that what happened? They died?" asked Adam.

"Well, by all logic it seems that they must have." Philip reached one hand helplessly toward Adam. "But— I think it's possible that there's more than logic at work. There is that legend, after all." He coughed delicately. "My dear boy, please come back from the edge. You're terrifying me."

Adam was silent for a long time. "You're right," he said at last, and turned away from the edge. "Let's go, then."

And again Philip was bewildered. Why did things always happen so quickly with Adam? "Go where?"

"To the Gray Lady. We capped a promised. And this Gray Lady might know what to make of it all." Adam whistled low, and Peat raised his head from the grass and came toward him. Philip moved out of the horse's way.

Carefully, they retraced their steps down the mountain.

Adam did not speak further until they reached the bottom. "We'll couch here for the night," he said. "You know, Mister Tutor, I used to think you were a stuffy pigwidgeon. But you're a rum old slyboots, after all."

Philip thought about that. "Thank you," he said.

Two days later, in the dark of night, Adam and Philip reentered Baytown and returned Peat to the stable. They'd had a rough trip back; the pups had trailed them—supporting Adam's theory that they weren't afraid of horses and it *was* Snowcap's fury that had scared them off earlier. At various points during their journey, the men had resorted to running, swimming, swinging fiery sticks, and throwing clods of mud. The mud hadn't worked, but luckily the other things had.

Colin, the under-gardener (who'd been arrested in England for cutting a rich man's trees and stealing the wood), had been temporarily promoted to horse groom, and after Adam peeked in and satisfied himself that Colin was doing an adequate job, he and Philip snuck away in a boat they nabbed off the beach. (Philip left a note that they would return the boat as soon as possible, but as the note blew away—and the owner couldn't read, anyway—the boat was considered stolen, and the Colay were of course blamed for its disappearance.) Philip and Adam knew that Colin would wonder who had returned Peat. But they wanted to see the Gray Lady before they spoke to anyone in town; they wanted to hear more of the story of the Rebellion before they tried to tell their people what had happened on the cliff, for they sensed the stories—the Rebellion and the cliff—were intertwined, and if they understood one, they might understand the other, too. They depended upon this: that the two stories would somehow explain each other.

Can two girls become hawks? Not long before their standoff on the cliff, Lucy would have said *no*. There are many who don't believe in magic; but there are others who only *seem* not to believe. Sometimes, in deepest peril, their belief can blossom, and for the length of a silvery moment, magic can become the most real of real things.

People still argue about what happened on the cliff that day. But Adam and Philip swear that this is what they saw: on a high cliff at the top of a mountain, two girls stood, one with a baby in her arms, and they stared longingly into the empty sky. Then they were gone, and two hawks soared up and up.

38

WHAT THEY DIDN'T SEE

What Philip and Adam didn't see, what they would've seen if they had lingered at the cliff for a few hours, what would've truly terrified them and made them postpone visiting the Gray Lady—and what would've convinced them beyond a doubt that something magical was going on—was this: in the roiling green waters of Botanist's Bay (or the Bay of Oddities) as the sun set, one of the two pink alabaster rocks in the shallows—the smaller, hunched one—began to transform. It looked like a lit candle with wax dripping down its side or, more closely, like a block of ice sitting in sunshine when the temperature is finally just above freezing. The stone began to bead up and the outer layers dripped into the waters of the bay. As the alabaster *melted*, the form of a man began to emerge. The expression on his face was strained in agony more than a living person ever should endure.

It was Renard, turning back from rock to human form. From the looks of it, he had pitted his own spells and willpower against the spells and willpower of the bay itself—and won. The water rushed away from him and he stood, wavering a bit, on a sandy bar. He glanced disdainfully at the tall, thin rock next to him; turned his back on it and staggered toward the shore, the water returning to its natural path behind him. When he reached the shore, the bay was roiling again, and Renard collapsed on the beach. The transformation had taken a toll. When he finally awoke, he lurched painfully back toward Baytown, resting often and long, and slowly gaining strength as he traveled. It took him almost a week to get back. The pups were afraid of him and stayed away.

No one witnessed this transmogrification—neither Philip nor Adam, neither Lucy nor Snowcap—no one but some seagulls and a family of loons, and they weren't telling.

39

THE DESERT PHILOSOPHERS

If asked to describe their journey from the Cliff of Good Hope to the desert, the girls couldn't have said much. But they remembered. They remembered jumping, falling, feeling the air rise up as if to receive them. They remembered strong wind in their faces and bright sun in their eyes. Tired shoulders. And laying down heavy burdens. Instead of trees, streams, and rocks, they recalled the land as a whole piece of cloth, as one might describe the patterns on a quilt, or the colors on a map.

And then their memories got fuzzy. The next thing they knew, they were sprawled on desert sand, Rob tucked between them, just north of three wide hills.

Their shoulders prickled and itched deep under the skin, in the bones. It seemed to be late in the day—or maybe the next day, they couldn't tell—and they felt more stiff and sore than they'd ever felt before. A young man stood in front of them, in a gray robe hooded and belted to keep out sun and sand.

"Welcome," he said warmly in Colay. His voice sounded like cinnamon.

Lucy sat up. "Are you a desert philosopher?" She picked up Rob and held him out expectantly.

But the man did not take the baby. "You must be from the islands. That's what we're called there. Philosophers. And you—" He turned to Snowcap.

"Anglish," she said.

"Huh. There's a tale here." He glanced up at the fading sun. "Please come with me and have supper, and we can share stories."

Lucy continued to hold out the baby. "He won't wake up. Help him. Please!"

The young man bent over to examine Rob. "A boy from the islands?"

Lucy knew what he was asking. "He started to turn, right after he was born, but I—he turned back."

The man stared at her. She tilted her face away, but he watched her closely as he spoke. "You know what's wrong. The stone is calling to him."

"You mean he's turning into a statue?" Snowcap asked, and Lucy closed her eyes.

"No." The man looked surprised. "I mean he misses the stone, and in a way, it misses him. In the woods and the desert, you're never as close to the stone as you are on the islands. There's none on Tathenn, you know."

"How can he miss stone?" Snowcap asked suspiciously.

Lucy, eyes still closed, put her hand on the luck pouch and considered how many times she'd touched it, how important that link to her home had been to her. And she'd taken Rob away from all that. Even as she grasped the lifestone, she could hear the man's voice, warm and calming. "People belong with their land. Especially now, when the land and the people are both so confused and angry."

Lucy opened her eyes. "What do we do now? We can't go back."

"Can't?" he said sharply. "Be careful about that word. It has a way of coming true. Walk with me. I think we can help him."

The young man pulled off his hood. His brown hair twisted in braids down his back. Lucy looked into his face and admired his firm jaw and strong white teeth; Snowcap liked his high cheekbones and steady gaze. He was tall for a Colay and brown as a roasted walnut, and he smelled like sweet milk and fennel. At that moment, they both decided to trust him.

The young man began to walk toward the first of the three low hills, from which a thin river of smoke curled up into the evening sky. Lucy and Snowcap followed. He said, "I am interested to hear why you two travel together, and to such a remote spot."

"You see," said Snowcap, "we need–"

"May I ask a question?" Lucy interrupted.

He nodded.

"How did you know we were coming?"

"I saw you in a dream. I saw your hand."

Lucy swung her hair forward to cover the mark.

"You misunderstand," he said. "This hand." He touched her fingers, which were aching again. Lucy jerked away.

Snowcap tried to fix the awkwardness. "I should introduce us." She thought of how her parents would have acted, what the proper etiquette would be—and then she realized her parents wouldn't have known the proper etiquette, being servants and convicts, after all; so she decided to simply say what seemed right. "I'm Snowcap. This is—"

"Lucy. And this is Rob."

"Pleased to know you. I'm called Beno."

"Oh!" Lucy had presumed, from the way Amarrah had spoken (lovingly and a bit longingly) that Beno was her husband, or her companion. But this young man couldn't be any older than Adam. "Amarrah sends you greetings. She says—she hopes to see you soon."

Beno again looked surprised. "Thank you."

"Amarrah?" asked Snowcap.

"The Lady on the Gray Mountain." Lucy wanted to know, but didn't think it polite to ask Beno, who Amarrah was to him.

Snowcap had no such reservations. "How do you know the Gray Lady?"

He gave a gentle smile that began and ended in his eyes. "She's my mother. Let us hurry home now, and we will settle the baby, and I will tell my story and you will tell yours."

My mother, echoed Lucy.

Snowcap echoed, *Home.*

40

A Woman May, on Occasion, Be Wrong

Soon the girls arrived at a series of low mud huts connected like a sprawling, many-roomed house. The building looked out at the desert, which was remarkably full of life. The hills themselves were old and flat, covered with rocks, mud, and small plants. As Beno explained, the desert philosophers cultivated gardens near the small springs at the base of the hills, and they raised goats on the slopes; the girls could see other people coming in with flocks. The "hut-warren," as Snowcap immediately dubbed it, sat partway up the most southern of the hills, backed against the wall of a low cliff.

Beno disappeared into one of the huts and came out

with a small sack. As he poured its contents carefully on the ground, stones spilled out—stones of all colors and textures—some shiny, some dull, some crystalline, some metallic, some smoothed by the sea, some crumbling, some dense and strong. Lucy gripped her luck pouch and the one stone left inside it.

"Hmm. I was sure I had some lifestone in here," said Beno. "I collect stones. One of every type I can find. Here it is!" He chose a piece of sharp, transparent stone the size of Lucy's big toe. "Look at this." He held it up to the light, and there inside the stone shimmered a tiny, perfect rainbow. Snowcap's eyes grew round, for she'd never seen such magic before; but Lucy nodded. Her father had told her the miniature rainbow was a sign of good lifestone, carve-able and true.

Beno turned his attention to Rob. Lucy held him out again, and this time Beno took the baby. "I heard a story about this once," he murmured. "Stone calls to stone." He cradled Rob in one arm and jiggled the stone in his free hand. "But what do we *do* with it?"

Lucy stared into her brother's sleeping face and saw only—stillness. She felt sick. She couldn't save him; she'd done everything she could think of, and it wasn't enough.

Then she raised her head and saw Snowcap also watching the baby, her face as strained and desperate as Lucy's. And when Snowcap raised *her* head, a powerful look flashed between the girls, quick as a thrown rock. Lucy gasped from the jolt of it. She had seen that Snowcap cared about them: Rob *and* Lucy.

When Lucy gasped, Snowcap took a step forward to catch her. But it wasn't necessary; Lucy staggered and straightened. Still, Snowcap was struck that she'd *wanted* to catch Lucy, that she hadn't wanted her to fall. For so long there'd been only anger. She thought she'd never feel anything else after her parents died, and here she was, feeling sorry for someone, and feeling regret, and helpfulness, and—and love. But the horrible part was—she looked back at Rob—it was too late again.

Lucy didn't understand why, but she knew what to do. She opened Rob's swaddling. "Put it there."

Beno looked at Lucy quizzically, then placed the stone on Rob's bare chest.

They waited. Nothing happened.

Snowcap hiccuped, trying not to embarrass herself by crying. She wished Peat were there; she wanted comfort.

Lucy, too, wanted comfort, and she reached automatically to her luck pouch. But even as she slipped her fingers inside for the egg-shaped stone, she knew that there was something more she needed to do. What was it?

Then she realized: Just putting Beno's stone on Rob wasn't enough. She needed to talk with the stone, to convince it. She pulled hers out of its pouch and placed it just below Beno's so that the rainbow and the egg nestled together on Rob's motionless body. Lucy laid her hand over the two stones, closed her eyes, and conversed. As in the garden, she begged the stones to let Rob return, reminded them that he was innocent and—what's more—not theirs to keep. They were still angry about the magician who'd perverted their power, but she would help—*was* helping, even now.

The communication took some minutes. Beno and Snowcap heard none of it, but in watching Lucy's intense expression move from pleading to stern and then to tender, they knew that something was happening.

Suddenly Lucy pulled her hand away, her face startled and joyful.

Rob yawned.

Beno smiled broadly. Snowcap trembled and found she could not speak. Lucy swayed again, this time with the weight of happiness and a new discovery. She took Rob from Beno and cradled him. "Could I have done that before? In the woods?"

Beno touched her arm, and she didn't pull away. "Maybe. Maybe not. Some things work only when they should." The rainbow lifestone still radiated on Rob's chest, Lucy's opaque stone shining below it.

Rob opened his eyes.

Lucy glanced up at Beno, only to see an emotion flutter across his face that looked like pride and even a little fear.

"What's wrong?"

He shook his head. "Nothing." And they all watched Rob awaken.

While dinner cooked in large pots over three fires, the visitors rested nearby on stones that seemed placed there for that purpose. Beno sat with them.

"So," said Snowcap, stretching. "Tell us your story."

"Ask what you like," said Beno.

Snowcap didn't know what question to ask. Wasn't a story simply *told*? You didn't have to dig for the answers. She almost lost her temper, but then she reminded herself that he had helped to save Rob and she was a guest waiting for a free meal, so she bit her lip and was silent.

Lucy, however, had many questions stored up. "Why did you leave Sunset? Why didn't you stay to help there?"

"My mother's doubts sent me home."

"What do you mean?"

"She believed that she could help the islands–"

"She *did* help," said Lucy. "She helped my mother, and a lot of other people, too. Why didn't she tell me you were her son?"

He leaned back and watched the darkening sky. "Maybe she felt guilty. We came because we knew you needed help. But she feared that I would not survive on the islands, that I, like your men, would turn to stone. And maybe she was wrong. But as long as she believed, it might come true. So, I came back here, and she stayed to help."

Lucy frowned. "You came by boat?"

"What other way would I cross the water?" He quirked one eyebrow.

Lucy thought of her cousins, Branch and Brady, and their story about the Gray Lady, and of her own strange, mysterious trip with Snowcap from the Cliff of Good Hope. "I–well, I can *imagine* other ways to travel," she said.

"Good. So can I."

Just as supper was served, Rob started screaming with hunger, a joyous noise to Lucy and Snowcap. Rob hadn't eaten since before they climbed the mountain, whenever that was. Without a hint from Lucy, Snowcap ran and asked a woman for some milk and brought back a bladder. Lucy smiled her thanks.

The food was plain but delicious: mutton and soft flatbread; water and milk and cheese; and some late berries, tiny and blue and overripe, that neither Lucy nor Snowcap recognized but both happily ate. People materialized out of the huts and from the hills and gathered around the outdoor fires. They served themselves from the pots and baskets nearby. There were about one hundred people in all, Snowcap guessed, everyone brown-skinned like the Island Colay, and all—men, women, and children—wearing long robes. Lucy did not study the people; she fed the ravenous baby, sitting a short distance from the fires. Snowcap filled two bowls and brought one back to Lucy. Beno talked with several people quietly, then served himself a bowl of bread and mutton and sat with the girls to eat.

Many of the philosophers glanced over at the visitors, but no one else ventured near. "Why don't they come and talk to us?" Snowcap asked.

"They know that you'll talk when you're fed and rested. They're practicing patience."

"Oh," said Snowcap. "Is that something they practice a lot?"

"Not much more than anyone else," said Beno. "Though we do make a point of it on occasions like this."

"Politeness," said Lucy, who had quickly finished her own meal.

"True patience is something a little bit different," said Beno.

Snowcap scrunched her nose. "Are you all philosophers here?" she asked. "Who takes care of the goats?"

Beno laughed. "We're not all philosophers. And

even those who are also tend goats and raise crops. Philosophy isn't terribly practical." He finished his meal and rubbed his hands in the sand to clean them. "May I hold the baby?" he asked.

Lucy held out Rob.

Beno curled the baby into the crook of one arm and stroked his head. He bent over Rob and sang softly, in his warm Colay, a song with a meter and tune that sounded strange to Snowcap but familiar to Lucy:

Now the birds have gone to bed;
They lay down their weary heads.
When they sleep, they dream of you;
And they dream you dream them, too.
Close your eyes, and close them tight;
Like a bird, sleep through the night.
And when you sleep,
You'll dream you fly with golden wings;
When you dream, you will have wings.
You'll fly so high,
Your wings will touch the farthest sky,
And you'll wheel and soar so high, so high.

"How did you know?" whispered Lucy.

"Know what?" Beno rocked the baby.

Snowcap stared. "Will you teach me that song? I–I think he likes me to sing to him." She ducked her head, almost shyly.

"I'll teach you tomorrow, if there's time." He got up, still holding the baby, and tilted his head at the girls to follow him. They walked to the space in the center of the three fires, and as they walked, everyone stopped talking and watched them expectantly. Beno faced the people. "I introduce Lucy and Snowcap, and the baby Rob."

The people set their bowls aside and moved closer until they sat in a half circle around them. Beno seated himself behind the girls, Rob in his arms. Lucy and Snowcap looked out, wondering what to say to this patient crowd.

"Perhaps," Snowcap said, "you can ask us questions."

Thus, in the desert way, they shared their stories.

41

SOLVING THE PROPHECY

After Lucy and Snowcap had answered as many
questions as they could, and let people file past Rob and
look him over, they stopped talking. They had no more
to say.

An old man stood up. He was dressed all in gray, and
his gray hair was twisted in thin strands down his back.
When he stood, everyone looked at him. "Perhaps," he
said, "there are still questions that you hope we can
answer?"

Snowcap stepped toward him. "Are you in charge
here?"

"In charge?"

"Are you the—the Governor? The man in charge?"

He smiled. "No, she's not here just now."

Both girls waited for the old man to introduce himself, but he did not. In her mind, Lucy named him the Gray Man.

Snowcap plunged ahead. "I need to know—did I do the right thing to come here?"

The old man said, "Our understanding of *the right thing* may be very different than yours. To our thinking, you did the right thing by helping Lucy and Rob arrive here. They are very important to us."

Lucy was surprised—but not as surprised as Snowcap, who had never been told before that she was less important than someone else. She was silent.

Lucy spoke up. "Please. Now that I've brought Rob here, what do we do?"

"*Why* did you bring Rob here?" asked the old man.

"Because of the curse. And Beno's prophecy. Amarrah said—"

"Did she tell you to leave your island?"

Lucy hesitated. *Had* Amarrah said that? "No, not precisely. She said that *if* I left Sunset, I should come here. I thought"—her voice rose against her will—"I thought you would know what to do."

"Why would we know what to do?" he said calmly. "What do you *want* to do?"

Lucy felt like crying. She had done her job—she had brought Rob here—and these people didn't seem to know how to help her. She wanted to keep Rob safe; she wanted to help the other men and boys, but she didn't know how! "I want to go to sleep. I'm exhausted," she finally said. She couldn't think any further ahead.

Beno stepped forward. He put one hand on Lucy's shoulder as he held the baby with the other, and he spoke only to her, though loudly enough for everyone to hear. "It's true that when I went to Sunset I spoke a prophecy: that a child born on Sunset would save the people. But a prophecy is never absolute. It depends upon our own wills and upon circumstance."

"Your mother already told me that," said Lucy. She held out her hands to take Rob and go lie down.

But Beno cradled Rob and continued. "One person might believe my words meant that a child *yet to be born* would save the people; another might believe that I spoke of a child *already* born. Others might consider exactly *which* people will be saved."

Snowcap asked, "What's the point of a prophecy if it doesn't tell you anything you can count on?"

Lucy nodded. She had been thinking the same thing.

"A prophecy marks you," said Beno, "but it does not *make* you. It is the beginning of a path that you may choose to follow. Without my prophecy, would you have thought to save Rob, to come here?"

"Perhaps not," Lucy said softly. Beno put Rob in her arms, but he kept his hand on her shoulder. She did not attempt to leave. She stared down into the baby's peaceful face. "Why didn't Rob freeze in the garden?"

"Another question might be: why did all the others freeze?"

"Because—" Lucy stammered, "because the Anglish shaman cursed them. But Rob should have frozen, too."

"When you were in the garden, what did you tell him?"

Lucy remembered. "Not to freeze. That I wouldn't let him freeze. That it wasn't fair. And then . . ."

"Then?"

"I asked the stones."

"You believed you could—talk with the rocks?"

Nodding, Lucy realized that it had never occurred to her to think otherwise.

Snowcap interrupted. "So a prophecy comes true if you believe it, or doesn't come true if you don't? That's too easy."

"Has your journey been easy?" asked Beno. "A prophecy can convince you to do things. Such as—*you will be Governor one day*. Without believing, would you have come here? Or been so convinced that Lucy's duty was to help and protect you? And Lucy, if you didn't believe you had to bring your brother here, would you have been so . . . inclined to help Snowcap? And if you didn't both love Rob and believe he is special, would you have trusted each other at the cliff?"

The girls looked in each other's faces. Had they always needed each other to fulfill their prophecies?

Then many people were smiling and laughing and talking. Beno led the girls toward one of the entrances to the huts. "Now sleep," he said. "And sleep well." But before he left them, he said, "You didn't ask one important question: why *Lucy*?"

"What do you mean?" asked Snowcap. But Lucy already knew.

"Lucy believes and things happen. Why?"

Lucy thought back on her talk with Amarrah. How she had helped save Rob with her stone. The spells she had written and erased, and what had followed. She tensed, like a soaring hawk just before it plummets to its prey. Her mouth opened wide, but no sound came out.

"Yes, why Lucy?" Snowcap asked eagerly.

But Beno had already left, and Lucy turned away to put Rob to bed. So Snowcap's question remained unanswered.

The girls slept indoors for the first night since they ran away, under warm blankets on the raised floor of a small, cozy room that reminded Lucy of Amarrah's hut. Rob woke once in the night, begging for more milk, so Lucy fed him and then Snowcap sang him back to sleep.

They all woke late in the morning. When they went outside, they found Beno waiting, tossing pebbles idly down the slope. "I've brought you some milk," he said, "and bread for your breakfast. Most everyone else is already up and gone."

"Gone?" said Snowcap.

"Work. We rise early."

They sat on a big stone pile. "I'm watching goats today." Beno gestured at the animals nibbling grass out of the crevices in the rocks or resting in the dappled shade of shrubs. Lucy fed Rob and then laid him in a hollow next to a large rock, out of the wind and sun. She and Beno sat down in the light breeze and ate.

Snowcap stood and began hopping from rock to rock with flatbread in her hand. She teetered from one rock to another, balancing on her toes, playing a game with herself to jump from stone to stone without touching the ground. Graceful as always, she was very good at it.

As they lazily watched Snowcap, Lucy said, "Do you think I should have come here?"

"Maybe it's what you needed—to learn what you are. To learn that you need to go back." Beno took a bite of bread and Lucy waited, trying to be patient while he chewed. He gestured to Snowcap. "It's all about finding balance." Another bite, another pause. "Today you rest. Tomorrow you go back to Picle."

"What?" She jerked and the water skin sloshed over her shirt. Snowcap, too far away to make out the words, glanced back, overbalanced, and fell to the grass. She picked herself up and danced off as if she had fallen on purpose. In a second, she was back on the rocks with her arms out, teetering slightly.

Beno said, "I had a dream last night, and I don't know what it means. But I feel strongly that you must go to Picle, and as soon as possible."

"I can't go there just because you had a dream," Lucy said. She rolled a little piece of flatbread between her fingers and threw it out for the goats. Then she asked, "What *was* your dream?"

"Does it matter if you're not going to go?"

Snowcap flitted over, from rock to rock, and then floated down to earth. "What's the fight about?"

"There's no fight," said Lucy.

"I'm telling Lucy that you both need to go back to Picle." Beno took another bite.

"What?"

"Exactly my question," Lucy noted.

For a moment, no one spoke. They tossed bread out for the goats, Lucy and Beno rolling it in their fingers first and Snowcap simply flinging out little pieces as if she were skimming rocks.

When the bread was gone, Snowcap said, "Why?"

"Another dream," said Lucy. "But he won't explain."

The goats wandered off and spread out on the hillside.

"My dream," said Beno, pausing as if to dare anyone

to stop him, "was about two short swords."

(The girls both thought: *The stilettos!*)

"They fell to the ground," he continued. "But then one of them got up."

"By itself?" Lucy asked doubtfully.

Beno raised an eyebrow. "It was a dream. These things can happen. Then a man appeared carrying the sword. I couldn't see him well, only his stony hand gripping the scabbard. And his chest covered with iron circles."

("Buttons," breathed Snowcap.)

("Renard," breathed Lucy.)

"He was heading toward Picle."

Snowcap stood up.

"He was heading toward Baytown."

Lucy stood up.

"It's not a good dream, that stony man. I don't understand all the details, but it worries me."

The girls nodded, wide-eyed. It was time to go back.

They did not wait until the next day. Instead, they rested through the morning, packed food and water, and ate another quick meal. Beno walked them down to the foot of the hills. He bade them a safe journey.

"Thank you for helping Rob," said Lucy, "but–"

"But we don't know what to do when we get there," finished Snowcap.

"Why not tell everyone your stories?" he said.

Lucy wondered, *Could it be as simple as that? Or as complicated?*

"It won't fix everything," Beno told them. "But it is a beginning."

"You didn't answer the question from last night:

why Lucy?" Snowcap persisted. "Why do things happen when she believes them?"

"Not just anything. Things to do with the stones, with our islands." He waited, but Lucy didn't speak. "Lucy knows."

Snowcap turned to her, and Lucy found herself looking into the blue eyes of her unexpected ally. She remembered Amarrah's words and decided to make her claim. "I'm—a shaman."

"A what?" Snowcap swiveled her head from Lucy to Beno and back again. "You mean a magician? Like Renard?"

"No. They're completely different things. I know that now."

"You just need to believe it," said Beno. He kissed the three of them on the forehead, a good-bye that they all hoped was not forever.

42

PHILIP AND ADAM'S VOYAGE

After they had returned Peat to his stable and borrowed a boat, Adam and Philip had rowed to Sunset. Or rather: Adam rowed to Sunset. To his credit, Philip tried to help as much as he could, but his help wasn't worth much. As they rowed, Philip recalled a poem from his childhood, and he made up a tune to the words as he recited:

Begin, be bold, adventure to devise.
He who defers his words too many days,
Dumbly waits for ships at unmapped bays
Till the tides and tales that pulled him there be gone,
Which run, and as they run, forever shall run on.

It was by a famous poet (named Smiley? Scowly? He wasn't sure). At nine years old, one rainy morning, he had pored over it in his father's library, desperate to memorize it before his harsh tutor arrived and commanded him, under pain of the rod, to recite it. Under the tutor's baleful glare, Philip had faltered and forgotten, but now he remembered. He was not quite certain about all the words, but he knew they were close. He had the ideas right, anyway. He matched his meter to Adam's paddling, his voice almost lost under the loud, slow sound of the surf and the calls of the gulls.

Adam and Philip did not arrive at Sunset until just before dawn. They avoided the Colay village—the villagers, they knew, would not be happy to see Anglish men—and beached their boat in a deserted little bay to the north. From the bay, they followed Lucy's directions and walked toward the Gray Mountain; when they reached it, they walked upward until they found a path that switched back and forth above the village. The path ended at an old cemetery: There was an archway, tart apple trees, long grass, burial mounds. Statues. Everywhere statues. The only sounds were distant birds and Philip's gasp.

They stood for a long time, looking and looking. The statues were so fragile and lifelike, Philip thought they were the most beautiful carvings he'd ever seen, truly works of art. Except . . . except not art, he knew, and therefore also the most frightening things he'd ever seen. He found himself searching for a man who looked like Lucy.

"This way," said Adam. "There's a path leading out."

"Where?"

"To the Gray Lady, I hope."

They followed the path until it opened onto a clearing, and there they saw a hut. No one was at home. They sat down outside the hut and waited, exhausted. After a short time, they dozed in the sun.

Mid-morning, Philip awoke to find a brown goat licking his face with its dry tongue; when he jumped in surprise, he bumped against Adam and woke him up, too. They looked up and saw the Gray Lady coming down a path with a basket on her head. She did not seem surprised to see them. As she neared, she lowered the basket, and both Adam and Philip recognized the plants she carried as ones that grew on Tathenn, but neither knew of any practical uses for them. The Gray Lady turned from the men, tied the plants in little bundles, and hung them from pegs inside her hut.

When she came back outside, she asked, "Would you like some tea?"

Adam said, "Yes, thank you" in his most polite Colay, but Philip blurted, "You don't even know who we are."

She shook the twigs and dust out of her tunic and smoothed it with her hands. "I assume you are Anglish. And I assume that you come with news, probably of my young friends."

"Yes, we are," said Philip, "and yes, we do." He would have gone on, but the Gray Lady shook her head.

"Tea first." She went inside and brewed the tea while the goats ate energetically in the clearing and chased one another. She came out carrying two bowls of tea, set them in front of Adam and Philip, and went back inside.

She came out again with her bowl, sat down on the grass, took a drink, and said, "Tell."

"We do indeed have news of Lucy and the baby . . ." Philip faltered. Suddenly he didn't know where to begin: there was too much to tell. He turned to Adam. "That is . . ." He sagged. "Adam can tell it much better than I can."

But Adam could not. "Truth is, we don't know exactly what happened. They jumped off the cliff—and the birds flew up—and we never saw them in the water—but how could they . . . ?"

"Hmm. Maybe you should start at the beginning." The Gray Lady leaned forward, rested her chin on her knuckles, and waited.

So Adam told the whole story, while Philip added comments. And when they finished, it was time for lunch. The Gray Lady said, "I'll think about all of this while you go out to the garden and bring me some greens." She gestured westward. "You can't miss it." Then she handed them a large bowl. Adam and Philip looked at each other, shrugged, and went out to the garden.

When they returned, the Gray Lady had made more tea. She looked over the greens. "I think there are some very good possibilities here."

"But what do you think happened to them?" asked Adam.

"We have to wait to see the ending," said the Lady. "Drink up. Good leaves."

When they had drunk deeply, and Philip felt so comforted that he began to wonder if the tea were drugged, the Lady set down her tea bowl. "People meet their destinies every day, but rarely do they understand them."

Philip squinted, feeling that everything people said recently was a little blurry. Or maybe he was a little blurry. "Whose destiny do you mean? Snowcap's or Lucy's? Or Rob's?"

"All of them," she said.

"Can you tell us the story of the Rebellion?" asked Philip.

"I think you already know that story."

"No, the real story," he said. "The truth."

The Gray Lady told it this way: first they ate lunch, which included the greens Philip and Adam had gathered; then she worked in her garden; then she milked her goats, showing Adam (who was very interested) and Philip (who was appalled by the procedure) how it was done; then she made supper. As the sun was setting and the air grew colder, the Gray Lady motioned Philip and Adam into her hut. They all sat on the floor and wrapped themselves in blankets. In the glow from the fire outside the door, the Gray Lady began:

"Some of the Anglish hated the Colay, and some ignored the Colay. Those that hated plotted for their demise, and those that ignored believed anything said about them, because they didn't care enough to search out the truth. An Anglish man named Mark the Ham hated the Colay and wanted to be king—even though this land has never had a king and does not want one. But one of the people he chose to help him was smarter than he was. And he was able to control Mark the Ham, like—"

"A cat with a mouse?" asked Philip.

"More like the stone controls the sculptor, and the

sculptor might—unless he is very good and very humble—never know it. Or the way a child plays with an ant, laying twigs and pebbles to direct its path, the ant never knowing that there is an intelligence—perhaps even a malevolent one—behind the maze it follows.

"But both men made a fatal mistake. They believed so much in their own power, they thought someone small could not pose a threat."

Afterward, Philip felt like a blind man who begins to make out shadows on a wall. They still didn't know *how* Sir Markham had killed the Governor and his wife, but perhaps they didn't need to, if they knew *why*.

This knowledge, however, did not make Philip feel better. What could be done in the face of such evil and catastrophe? The O'Kellys' murders involved not just Snowcap, or Adam and Philip, or Sir Markham and Renard, but everyone in Tathenland, all the English and the Colay.

Adam asked, "What should we do? What *can* we do? How can we make things right?"

The Gray Lady spread out her hands. "You can't change what's happened. But you can change the future, if you tell the truth about the past. Go back to Picle, to Baytown, and meet Lucy and Snowcap when they return. When the girls tell the story of what happened to them and what they've learned, be there to support them. And if they should not return, tell their stories for them. The history of a place is important to its people—even a small place like ours."

"Truly," said Philip, "we are so small that we don't even exist. I mean to say, when I lived in England, I never saw any books about Tathenland, no maps, nothing."

"So our stories are even more important—because we're the only ones to tell them."

Philip squinted at a minor epiphany, the first really in his life. He saw that the stories of the staged Rebellion and the assassination, the kidnapping attempt, and the rescue of the baby, and all the rest that had happened were all one story—part of one giant and elaborate tapestry—and they were all important. They must be told properly.

He blinked his eyes, refocused on the world around him, and saw that the Gray Lady was watching. "So who are you?" she asked.

He replied, "My name is Philip. They called me Robbing Parsons. I'm a thief."

"Ah," said the Lady. "The Tutor."

"Yes," said Adam. "And"—he had to switch to English to say it—"a smashing good speller."

43

RETURN TO BAYTOWN

The next morning, after a cozy sleep on the floor of
the hut, Philip and Adam went to visit Lucy's mother.
They brought hard news. Her daughter had, after all,
jumped off a cliff holding the baby she'd thought had
turned to stone.

When they reached the village, two tiny girls ran up
to them, yelling, "What are you? Are you *men*?"

"Anglish!" called a woman, in warning and fear, and
the little girls immediately shrieked in terror and ran
away. Philip and Adam were alone. The huts stood open,
but no one came out. No sound now but the rustling
trees. No movement save the waving of mended nets

and clean laundry in the breeze.

Philip cleared his throat and spoke loudly and slowly, "We . . . come . . . in . . . peace."

Adam snorted. "We're here with news about Lucy. We wish to speak with her mother. We're unarmed." He waited, and still there was nothing. "We come from the Gray Lady."

A thin, sickly woman materialized in one of the doorways. "I'm Lucy's mother. Where is she?" And suddenly the doorways were filled with the faces of girls and women.

Philip and Adam told their story to all the women and girls of Sunset as they sat around the common fire. There were many questions, big and small: What does Snowcap look like? Why is Renard a servant to Sir Markham when he is so clearly the master? How big is a horse? How small are the pups? And what exactly happened on the cliff? The last answer they studied, detail by detail.

"This may be good news," breathed one woman.

"To have the power of birds. Who knew?" said another.

"I always thought that child had something in her."

"Yeah, a bad spirit," muttered an older girl seated next to Adam. Then she blushed. "I didn't mean that."

"Why not?" asked Adam. "She does have a lot of—spirit—in her."

"It's just not possible," declared an old woman.

"What's that, Bastia?"

"She flew? Off a cliff? Our Lucy? No, no, no. She's about the heaviest child I've ever seen. And I don't mean heavy like me," Bastia said, patting her belly. "How could she do it? Unless—" She shook her head dismissively. "Not Lucy."

"People sometimes do things we don't expect," said Adam.

Later, when they were ready to leave, Lucy's mother pulled them aside. "I need to know," she said. "Is Lucy angry with me?"

"Why would she be angry?" asked Philip.

"I didn't think—I didn't believe—I sent my baby away. I should have been the one to save him, but instead I sent him away to die." Tears filled her eyes, and Philip understood why she looked so fragile and sick.

Wanting to make her feel better, Philip said the first thing that entered his head. "Be strong. Regrets can kill you." It sounded pompous even to him.

"Really?" said Adam. "Do you know anyone who's died that way?" Philip stared at him. "Don't kick yourself," Adam translated. "Who knows what'll happen next. Could be something good."

"Thank you," Dara said. "When you go back to Tathenn, if you should see Lucy, tell her . . ." She trailed off.

"We will," said Adam.

The Gray Lady seemed to think they should spend one more night with her, so they did, working for her during the day and sleeping on the floor of her hut again, nestled next to warm goats. In the evening they shared stories. She told them about Tathenland and the Colay. Adam told about horses and about thievery in London. Philip tried to describe books.

The Gray Lady woke them early and told them it was

time to go. She'd had a dream; she was worried; they needed to return quickly.

"What dream?" asked Philip groggily.

"There is only one pink stone in the big bay. The other stone is awake."

"The *what* is *what*?" Philip was awake now, but confused.

Adam stood up and pulled on his trousers and shirt. "Sounds like Renard." He turned to the Gray Lady. "Will you come?"

"No. I'm needed here. The stones are very angry. They don't like being used in this way."

Philip shook his head to clear it. "The stones are angry?"

But Adam seemed to understand. "What can we do?"

"Nothing," said the Gray Lady. "Except help Lucy if she arrives."

"You mean Snowcap," said Philip. "As Child Governor, she can oppose—"

"I mean Lucy. She has . . ."

"Power over the stones?" Philip guessed.

"No, that's exactly what she does *not* have." The Lady paused, searching for the right word. "She has a connection."

"I think the land loves her," said Adam. "The way horses love Snowcap."

"Not love," corrected the Lady. "Belonging. Snowcap will play her part, certainly, in opposing Renard. But it is Lucy who needs to call the men and boys back."

"Back?" asked Philip.

"From the stones."

In the wee hours of the morning, Philip and Adam rowed to Baytown, leaving the boat where they had found it. The town was strangely, ominously quiet. They went to the stables and saw that Peat was well. They slept and waited there—Philip finding that close proximity to the beasts no longer bothered him—for the girls to return.

At noontime Colin, the under-gardener, came in to feed the horses—and yelped at the sight of the travelers. After they calmed him down, they convinced him to reveal what had happened since they left. Colin told them that the school was closed; the government was shut down; businesses were keeping haphazard hours, only the pubs still operating on their normal schedule. The town was in an uproar over the disappearances of its most important government officials: the Child Governor, the Protector, and the Minister of Transportation (Snowcap, Sir Markham, and Adam, respectively).

"And Renard?" asked Philip.

Colin stared. "He's gone missing again? But I saw him this morning, when he was speechifying about going off to the Colay Islands—"

Adam stood up. "Renard's here?"

"Well, yes, unless he's disappeared again like you just said."

"Tell us about Renard," said Philip. "When did he come back?"

"Oh, it's a very exciting story. He was captured by the Colay rebels, and they tried to put a hex on him, but he fought it off with his English power."

"His *what*?" said Adam.

"Or something like that. Anyway, he managed to escape, and walk back from the dark forest where they had kept him bound, and he reported with great sadness that Snowcap and Sir Markham were dead. He rallied the people to swear, in the memory of these good folks, that *we will not rest* until we have avenged their deaths!" Colin, exuberant and pink-faced, raised his fist high.

"Oh, my," said Philip. Adam shook his head slowly, as if his ears hurt.

Colin looked quizzically at Adam. "He didn't say what had happened to you."

"Well," said Adam. "As you can peep, I'm bang up."

"I'm fine, too," said Philip.

Colin turned to Philip in surprise. "You were gone?"

According to Colin, when Peat returned to the stable, they knew that he, too, had somehow escaped his Colay kidnappers and run home. Now the English were planning a raid on the Colay Islands, where they would take their own hostages. The Colay must not be allowed to raid Tathenn—or ever to stand on its shores—again. Colin's eyes flashed. "I'm going along on the attack," he said. "It's set for tonight."

"This is terrible," said Philip. "What can we do? Colin, you must realize that it's not true?"

"What do you mean? And how did you escape the savages?"

Philip, almost hysterical, cried, "We *didn't* escape them, and they're not—"

"Not now," said Adam. We'll tell the story tonight." He turned to Colin. "What time do you plan to sneak over to the islands?"

"At dark. Do you want to join us? We could always use more hands. One of our boats was stolen by the Colay—but we can budge you in somewhere."

"No. We just want to talk to you coves before you scour off," said Adam.

"A rallying speech?"

"Something like that."

"I'll spread the word," said Colin.

"But until then," said Adam, "we don't want to be palavered with. We'll couch in the stable till tonight."

"We need to rest. We're very tired," added Philip.

"Oh, of course," Colin replied. "I should think so, after escaping and all." And he shook their hands vigorously and left.

Philip looked at Adam. "I hope it works."

"What other chance do we have? We don't have enough of a gang to stop them. Just words."

"I only hope the story is strong enough."

"I doubt it will be, if it's only you and me that tell it." Adam slumped against a wall, and they continued to wait for Lucy, Snowcap, and Rob to return.

44

LUCY TELLS STORIES

The girls and Rob had, in fact, neared the city the same night as Philip and Adam. They had walked back through a still forest, undisturbed by wild pups—except for one important incident. On their first night in the forest, they had heard a snuffling and scratching just outside their circle of firelight. Snowcap picked up a stick to investigate and discovered an ugly, brown-and-gray one-eyed pup, as large as a possum, scrabbling in the dirt. When she got closer, he rolled over on his back and wriggled as if waiting to be scratched. So Snowcap did what she felt was right: she rubbed his belly and named him Dander. And in that moment, she acquired another companion. Despite Lucy's initial objections, Dander followed them home, heeling after Snowcap.

They slept on the forest side of the wall, surrounded by quiet. But when morning came, they could hear a disturbing hubbub and excitement on the other side, and they put off returning. Lucy dawdled over Rob's feeding; Snowcap was oddly slow at pulling the burrs out of Dander's coat. Then Rob cried and fussed, and the girls spent hours singing to him and rocking him. Of course, they all needed naps after their journey. And then supper. Thus they used up the day.

At dusk, the town hushed dramatically. Snowcap told Dander to wait there (and he lay down sulkily, as if he understood). Then she scaled the wall and peered over it. "No one!"

The girls both climbed over the wall and saw it was true: the town was deserted. But they could hear noise ahead of them, voices rumbling like thunder. They followed the sound. The voices grew louder and louder. At the harbor they saw a big crowd, so big it appeared to be all of the Anglish gathered together, all with stiff shoulders, angry backs, and hands in fists. The people faced the dock, on which Adam and Philip stood—and near them: Renard!

Lucy elbowed Snowcap and gestured. Snowcap followed her into the shadow of a doorway where they could hear and not be seen.

"Please listen!" Adam yelled. "What we've told you is the rum truth!"

But Renard's thin, sharp voice cut through Adam's. "Lies! Lies from a turncoat. Ask him how he survived in the woods. He *sold* us—he and that thieving schoolteacher—they sold us to the Colay! All for a little bit of gypsy-um!"

The crowd murmured in a way that sounded distinctly unfriendly.

Adam tried again. "Everything we tell you is true!"

"We've heard your story," said the miller (a murderer from Bournemouth).

The seamstress (a nimble-fingered pickpocket from Whitechapel) called out, "We don't believe you!"

And one of the fishermen (a brawny highwayman): "Where is the Child Governor? Where is this Colay girl you speak of?"

Snowcap elbowed Lucy this time, and they stepped out into the street as the Child Governor called out, "Here we are!"

People gasped, turned, and made way as the girls walked to the dock. Lucy carried Rob in her arms and tugged on her luck pouch; Snowcap marched like a general. Philip yelled, "Thank the heavens! You're safe!" And Adam's face shone.

Renard quickly rethought the situation. "Snowcap! I can't believe you've escaped! Or—*have* you?" His voice rose. "Perhaps you, too, are a traitor! With the Colay girl!"

Snowcap didn't bother to answer him. She climbed up on the dock next to Adam and Philip and faced the crowd. Lucy climbed up, too, and wedged herself next to Snowcap, her arms still wrapped around Rob and her hand reaching inside the luck pouch for courage. So many Anglish words were flying around her. And Renard stood so close and angry.

Snowcap spoke. "Renard is a liar and a murderer—"

"Perjurer!" screamed Renard. His right hand whipped out, the fingers straight and stiff.

"I can prove it!" Snowcap stood defiant, her eyes flaming.

Renard's outstretched hand seemed to suck in the light all around. It looked like a brilliant gem.

But before he could cast a spell, Lucy's hand shot out from her luck pouch and whipped the lifestone at him. She didn't think; she just threw. The stone cracked against the back of his hand with a loud, hollow sound. Then the stone fell to the ground like a small dead thing, and Renard's hand jerked to his chest with another hollow thunk. Renard quaked. His entire body roiled in great, racking shudders, each one slower and bigger than the one before. Then ripples, as if he were trying to move but couldn't, like a pudding being shaken.

And then he was still. Stone. Not the almost-man-shaped pink alabaster from the Bay of Oddities, but a perfectly formed stone Renard, of dun-colored gypsy-um remarkably free of impurities. As if sculpted by a skilled artist—no, not *sculpted* at all, but grown, like a flower. He wasn't trapped in the stone; he *was* the stone.

Lucy handed Rob to Adam and picked up her lifestone. She slid it back in her pouch.

The crowd was silent. Frozen. Aghast.

Snowcap turned to them and held out her hands. "My companion has a story to tell you. Everything she says is true." She turned to Lucy and spoke in Colay. "Please," Snowcap said. "Tell."

Lucy's story was more than words: it was her gestures, her tone of voice, her pauses for Snowcap to translate,

Snowcap's intense Anglish, the audience's passionate silence, all of these things and more. Words alone cannot convey this kind of telling; they can only sum it up.

Standing on the dock in Picle before all the Anglish, Lucy told the story of what *really* happened, as if she were knotting the threads and mending the holes in a large and broken net. She shook her hair away from her face and looked into the eyes of her listeners. Telling the truth of what happened, she felt a power as strong as a spell. The audience listened without interrupting, reaching for Lucy's every word. And when she ended the story and Snowcap echoed in Anglish—"and now we have returned here, to Picle, to Baytown"—Lucy threw out her arms, let go of the net, and watched it settle over the sea of listeners. They were caught up in her tale.

Then she moved backward in time and told a story that even Snowcap didn't know, a story that Amarrah had told her on the day that Rob didn't die, a story that Lucy had saved until the right time. Lucy told the story of how the islands rose from the sea, the people rose from the islands, and stories rose from the people. She told of curses that brought floods and storms and famines, sicknesses and deaths, and how the world righted itself eventually. Of people who tried to control the land but couldn't. Of people—a few, always only a few—who could speak with the land, who understood it, and the land belonged with them. Not *to* them, *with* them. Then she explained—as Amarrah had explained to her and as she now understood and believed—that curses grew from a desire to control—land and people—and thus they were never carved in stone. They could be changed.

Lucy's face moved in and out of the moonlight and

torchlight, and Snowcap found herself thinking, even as she was working hard to translate from Colay to English: *Slap or angel's kiss? Slap or angel's kiss?* The birthmark seemed to float back and forth between the two as Lucy spoke, until Snowcap thought that perhaps this face at this moment, enemy and friend, might be not only the most beautiful, but also the most terrifying she'd ever seen.

She did not realize that Lucy was thinking almost the same thing about her translator.

Finally, Lucy was too hoarse to speak any longer. She was empty, an unstrung net. She sank down on the dock, and Snowcap sat next to her. Rob, in Adam's lap, cooed. The crowd, released, breathed deeply and looked around, as if they were just waking up and wondering what to do with the newborn day.

Lucy opened and closed her right hand. It was finally warm. She had kept her word. Gift and promise.

And in each of the thirteen Colay Islands, the stone gardens sighed and began to move.

45

EPILOGUE

Poor Salter's nose was never the same, but he otherwise recovered, as did Lucy's cousins, Branch and
Brady, and all the other men and boys of the Colay
Islands—and, of course, Lucy's father, whose own hand
looked as good as new. Rob, the baby over whom such
fuss had been made, grew into a toddler, fighting his nap
and playing with bugs and putting questionable objects
into his mouth—happy and healthy and ordinary. His
family found him exceptional.

Across the Colay Islands, there was great rejoicing,
and then a lot of work to be done and adjustments to be
made. The three women who had learned to fish decided

they enjoyed it and kept on fishing even after the men returned. Lucy's father became a much quieter man. People adapted.

Meanwhile, Adam was appointed Protector of Anglish Tathenland (mostly, this meant he met with Colay elders to form new treaties and trade agreements), and Philip was appointed to a newly created position: Snowcap's Guardian. Both appointments were to last until Snowcap turned fifteen and officially became Governor.

Snowcap decided to sleep in the stables—until Philip insisted she come inside and use a proper bed. She obeyed (which showed how much she'd changed), but she brought Dander inside with her, and they visited Peat for hours every day. She could not bear to be away from these two companions.

Shortly after the girls returned from the desert, Snowcap issued a proclamation (in her own flawed, misspelled handwriting) stating that when she became Governor, she would share the duty with Lucy. People were shocked. *Snowcap* was going to *share*? They wondered if it were true that she'd been magicked, somehow. But eventually, in the way of things, they accepted her plan. Which is to say, they'd wait and see.

Lucy did not immediately accept the offer, but said she'd think about it and decide when she was fifteen. (It turned out that their birthdays were less than a month apart.) She returned to Sunset and began to study with Amarrah to be a shaman. Beno visited often. With Amarrah, Lucy studied herbs, stories, and patience; with Philip, who often rowed himself over, she learned English, including how to read and write. Adam came over whenever he could and studied with them.

After he taught Lucy each lesson, Philip would seat himself next to her at Amarrah's feet and listen to Colay stories until he could retell them without forgetting even a syllable. One day he thought to himself, *Who is to say that our books are better than her stories? Books are, all told, as faulty as memory.*

He stayed on in Piclebay (the new name for the capital of Tathenland) as Tutor. He did not become the wisest and most inspiring teacher who ever lived, but he tried much harder. And his students appreciated it. Children and grown-ups alike forgot that Philip's real name was Robbing Parsons, and he gained a new nom de plume, the first good one that he hadn't given to himself and the one that gave him the most genuine pleasure: "Mister Tutor."

Once again he decided to write something. A true story—a remarkable story of love and adventure. Not because he wanted to be a Famous Author, but because he had been present for many of the events—and he wanted to make sure that later historians would not get it wrong, as he once had. Philip wanted to write, in all its twists and intricacies, a story in which he was not the hero, not even a major character; for his most startling realization had been of his own smallness. He decided to tell a story without beginning or end. He would simply tell everything he knew: the truth, the rumors, the suspicions, the lies—for they had all, in their own way, happened.

Thus he sat down at his desk and began to write.

But what happened to Sir Markham and Renard?

When Renard transformed on the docks in Piclebay, he couldn't turn himself back. The land had turned against him, for he had never understood nor belonged to it. There he remained, smooth and dusky gray, an alabaster statue. Many people, when they found out what he had done, wanted to stone him, but as Adam pointed out, stoning a statue was a rather pointless gesture. Snowcap, after a night to think it over, took pity on Renard and asked Adam to decree that the statue be preserved as a reminder of their history. So it was moved just off the docks, and Adam built a little white fence and placed flowers and a bench around it. People sat on the bench on pleasant days while they waited for the fishermen to return. As a statue, Renard made a lovely centerpiece for the dock area, a thing of beauty.

When—as was bound to happen—Renard began to crumble, Amarrah came and fixed the broken pieces. But each time, she remade the statue a little different. She was the kind of artist who tinkers. She was less a sculptor than a net mender, a translator, a storyteller. Her talent was long and deep, like a stiletto.

In repairing, she made small adjustments. When Renard's fingers broke off, which happened early on, Amarrah re-created them, but with ever-so-slight alterations. Instead of grasping and clawing, the hands now looked soft and open, giving; birds liked to land on them. When a hailstorm dug large pits in his crooked back, she took the opportunity to smooth out the hump so that—as she explained to Snowcap—he wouldn't be in such constant pain. ("He was in pain?" asked Snowcap. It had never occurred to her.) Eventually, between the crumbling stone and the patient healer, Renard transformed again. Amarrah put laugh-wrinkles in the folds around his eyes, pulled his eyebrows into a rounded arc, eased the tight anger in his neck and shoulders, and (the most noticeable change by far) reshaped his scream of anger and fear into an openmouthed smile that looked suspiciously like joy. He became, in stone, the man he really should have been in life, and children loved to dress him up in flowers and play around him.

Renard has not yet become flesh again—nor has Markham returned from the sea. But if they do someday return, perhaps they will be different than they were. Perhaps better. After all, everyone can transform, everyone can change. Everyone.

The End

Afterword:
Author Note on History

What in all this story is true? Tathenland, as you might guess, does not exist on any map, nor are there any written histories of it. But the country to which the colonists were originally headed, America, is mentioned in most reputable history books. And the English did send many criminals there as punishment. In fact, by 1775, the year of the voyage in this story, nearly 50,000 convicts had been transported from England to America, most of them to Virginia or Maryland, but some also to New York, the Carolinas, the West Indies, Bermuda, and so on. As historian Roger Ekirch has shown, most convicts were men between fifteen and twenty-nine years of age and were lower class—laborers or poor. But mixed in with these were women (between ten and twenty percent), young teenagers, old people, artisans, skilled tradesmen, and even a few of the aristocracy.

English law at the time was quite harsh—and somewhat capricious. Certain crimes that are considered serious offenses today were taken lightly then, and some of today's petty crimes were then considered serious offenses. Attempted murder, for example, was considered a misdemeanor. But stealing a silver spoon was grand larceny, punishable by transportation or even death. Crimes that could get you transported to America included stealing (even food, even if you were poor and starving), forgery, picking pockets, and damaging property. If you were caught, you would be arrested and tried in court. If the court found you guilty and sentenced you to transportation, you would be sent to gaol (jail) until a ship could be assigned to transport you. You might sit in gaol for several months, or even a year, waiting; and English gaols were dirty and dingy, with little food or warmth, often overrun by rats and diseases. Death rates were high. On average, ten percent of prisoners may have died in gaol of contagious illnesses, especially smallpox and "gaol fever" (a horrid form of typhus spread by lice).

Ship owners were paid a set fee for each convict they transported, and they were allowed to sell the convict into servitude in the American colonies for additional money. The catch was that they had to take whichever criminals they were given, and some were unlikely to get a good price; especially hard to sell were women, old people, sick people, and violent criminals (Ekirch 89).

The convicts were chained into the bottoms of crowded, smelly boats and brought across the Atlantic to the ports of the American colonies, where they were sold as indentured servants—meaning, they were owned for a certain amount of time (most often, seven years) by the person who had bought their labor. After that time, they were set free. Indentured servants were certainly better off than slaves kidnapped from Africa, for they had the hope of eventual freedom for themselves and their children. Still, many indentured servants did not always consider this bright spot.

Transportation of criminals to America began in about 1715 and was curtailed in spring 1775. After a certain rebellion you might recall from history books, Britain began searching for a new destination for their convicts. (Eventually they settled upon the colony of Australia.)

For further reading on the transportation of criminals to America, see especially:

Ekirch, A. Roger. *Bound for America: The Transportation of British Convicts to the Colonies, 1718–1775.* Oxford: Clarendon Press, 1987.

Shaw, A.G.L. *Convicts and the Colonies: A Study of Penal Transportation from Great Britain and Ireland to Australia and Other Parts of the British Empire.* London: Faber and Faber, 1966.

I owe these two books a huge debt, both for how they have broadened my knowledge of colonial life and for the specific ways they have contributed to this novel. Much thanks to you, Ekirch and Shaw and all brave tellers of history! Long may historians prosper!

SPECIAL NOTES:

Adam's "Virginny" song (Chapter 25) is a folk song slightly adapted from the lovely piece on Martin Carthy's *Crown of Horn* album (which is also quoted in Ekirch's book). Other songs are original. Philip's poem (Chapter 42) is loosely adapted from a poem by Abraham Cowley, a seventeenth-century English author.

Some characters were inspired in part by real historical figures. Adam's grandmother is named after a real convict: Mary Young (alias Jenny Diver), whose gang smuggled her back from the colonies. "Robbing Parsons" was the son of a baronet, transported for forgery. And there really was a woman who tried to get herself transported so that she could accompany her convict husband to the colonies (her name was Elizabeth Martin, and her arrest did not end as fortuitously as our Nora O'Kelly's did). A few convicts, like Adam's brothers, volunteered for medical experiments in order to avoid transportation. And London's criminal class did, in fact, create their own dialect, called flash-cant—the language of thieves. (You can find good examples of this language in a "Canting Dictionary," by N. Bailey of London, included in his 1737 *Universal Etymological English Dictionary*—and available on the Internet, transcribed by Liam Quin.)

Finally, lifestone is not actually a real stone in our world, though many of its properties are based on the mineral we know as gypsum, or—in its purest and most carve-able form—alabaster. The key difference between Tathenland's "gypsy-um" and our gypsum is that in Tathenland the stone is more powerful, more *itself*, than anywhere else in the world. For example, it is a fact in our world that gypsum can be turned into a powder (by heating) and then "reconstituted" by adding water, but this reconstitution is long and slow, happening through the natural processes of evaporation and flooding.